I0521327

Storylandia

The Wapshott Journal of Fiction

Issue 28

Storylandia, Issue 28, The Wapshott Journal of Fiction, ISSN 1947-5349, ISBN 978-1-942007-23-4 is published at intervals by the Wapshott Press, now a 501(c)(3) nonprofit, PO Box 31513, Los Angeles, California, 90031-0513, telephone 323-201-7147. All correspondence can be sent to The Wapshott Press, PO Box 31513, LA CA 90031-0513. Visit our website at www.WapshottPress.org to learn more. This work is copyright © 2019 by Storylandia. The Wapshott Journal of Fiction, Los Angeles, California. Copyright © 2018 Jennifer Wilson and is reprinted here with the copyright owner's permission.

Storylandia is always seeking quality original short stories, novelettes, and novellas. Please have a look at our submission guidelines at www.Storylandia.WapshottPress.org or email the editor at editor@wapshottpress.org

Donations happily accepted at donate.wapshottpress.org

Cover: Photo by Jennifer Wilson

Storylandia

The Wapshott Journal of Fiction

Founded in 2009

Issue 28, Winter 2019

Edited by Ginger Mayerson

Make Me Disappear

By Jennifer Wilson

Make Me Disappear

by
Jennifer Wilson

Make Me Disappear

*The brave dies perhaps two thousand deaths if he's
intelligent. He simply doesn't mention them.*
~Ernest Hemingway

1

The pocketknife had been a gift on her fourteenth
birthday.

Mabel had longed for one ever since her foster
brother John—an eagle scout with a sash full of
badges—had received his own. She had been fascinated
with the various tools that he could pull from it, from
a corkscrew to a tiny screwdriver to diverse blades,
and had watched with envy each time he brought it
forth from his pocket, slicing through tape-encased
packages with practiced ease and carving rough
animals from raw blocks of wood.

Her current foster mother, Karen (her own
mother had abandoned her many long years before to
a meth and petty theft habit), had rolled her eyes at
the gift, saying that there was no reason for a girl to
have a pocketknife at all, but John had wanted her to
have it and his will had prevailed.

"She'll probably cut her own nose off, for God's
sake," Karen said.

"I'll teach her to use it properly, Mom," John

answered, patting Mabel on the shoulder.

And he had, showing her how to open and close it so that it didn't snap on her fingers, and instructing her to always point the blades away from herself. She had imagined that she would use her knife in the same way John used his, but in the end the only things she seemed capable of carving were sticks into sharpened points and her initials in the bark of the ancient live oak tree in the back yard. Still, she carried the knife with her everywhere, the weight of it in her pocket giving her a sense of security and protection— from what she did not know, exactly.

"I'll be going away to college in a few weeks," John said to her as they sat on the back porch in the late afternoon sunshine of a warm summer day. "I just want you to know that if you ever need me, just call, okay? I'll only be two hours away."

"Okay," Mabel said, leaning into him for a hug. "I'll miss you."

"I'll miss you too, little sis."

When the day had come for him to leave, Karen had sobbed loudly and dramatically, and her foster father, Gary, was withdrawn and silent. The remaining week of summer passed slowly, and she spent it in solitude, vaguely dreading the coming school year. She was an average student, feeling unmotivated to do more than the bare minimum, and most subjects simply didn't hold her interest. Friends were hard to come by, as she didn't seem to fit in to any particular group at school, so the anticipation of seeing friendly faces again was, by and large, nonexistent.

She was not a particularly unhappy girl, however, though prone to bouts of ennui and melancholy. Being content in her aloneness and unused to any surfeit of attention, she spent much of her time outside, exploring the middle-class suburb of Tulsa she inhabited and communing with nature. She enjoyed reading and visited the library frequently, finding friends in the books she read and comfort in the knowledge that she was not so very unique as it seemed sometimes.

It was a sunny October Friday, the day John died. A texting teen swerved across the line on the road as he was coming home from college for a visit and the impact killed him instantly. Mabel would always remember the day; how the leaves were just beginning to change on the pear trees that lined the sidewalk, the sky clear and blue as she walked home from school.

She heard Karen's wailing before she reached the path that led to the front door, a high-pitched keening that raised the hair on the back of her neck and begged her to run in the other direction rather than discover the reason for such a noise. Against her instincts, she turned the knob on the front door with a trembling hand and was met by Gary, his face ashen and grim as he told her the news.

The tears didn't come then.

Nor did they come later, when she viewed John's body in the casket at the funeral. It didn't look like him anyway, stiffly posed and oddly-hued. Karen sat slumped in the pew of the church, heavily tranquilized so as to not make the scene any worse than it was. Gary, broken and silent, shook hands with family and friends. John was popular and well liked, and the procession took a long, wearying time.

Home was no refuge. The people kept coming, bringing pie and cake and casseroles that no one wanted to eat—more food than could possibly be consumed by anyone with an appetite. It fell to Mabel to open the door and greet the mourners, as Karen had taken to her bed and Gary was usually in a drunken stupor by three in the afternoon. She did her best to make conversation, but the forced words fell from her mouth woodenly. She didn't know what to say anyway.

The weeks passed. Karen did not get out of bed and refused to eat. Gary called the paramedics and they came, ambulance wailing, and took her away, strapped to a stretcher. Mabel didn't cry then either. Instead, she cleaned the house obsessively, vacuuming and dusting, washing dishes and clearing away the take-out boxes that littered the living room.

One night, a month after her world fell apart, with Gary passed out on the couch and Karen in the hospital again, being tube-fed the will to live, Mabel sat on the back porch where she and John had talked so often about their plans for their individual futures. Pulling her pocketknife from her pants, she carefully opened the blade and viewed it with a detached thoughtfulness. She slid it gently over her arm, watching as it scraped the fine hairs neatly off her skin, tracing it over the blue veins that stood out in stark contrast to the pale ivory of her complexion.

The emptiness welled up within her chest, threatening to choke her, and she lifted her face to the sky, full of stars twinkling with indifference. Her grief seemed to fill the universe, spiraling out from her soul and sweeping across the expanse. She felt she might be suffocating from the pressure building within her, longing for a release she did not know how to give.

Again and again she caressed her arm with the knife, each time pressing incrementally harder, rocking slightly as she sat on the concrete stoop, desperate to feel something besides darkness and relentless waves of nothing. Her mind was a mass of confusion.

You're not human at all. The thoughts came

unbidden. *Everyone can tell, you're a fake. Fake! Where are your tears, Mabel? You're heartless, that's what you are. John loved you but you have no heart. Fake!*

She shook her head violently, trying to suppress the voice.

She pressed harder.

Suddenly and silently, the blade carved a tidy line along her forearm, a thin ribbon of crimson springing up from the skin. Mabel made a small noise of surprise and stared at the wound, breathing hard. The ribbon became a trickle that ran down her arm and onto the stoop in thick, heavy drips. The puddle glistened darkly in the moonlight.

Swiftly—before reason could protest—she slid the knife over and over in parallel tracks along her skin, panting and stifling the urge to cry out until the pain rose up and eclipsed the deep nothingness for a brief, delirious moment. Dropping the pocketknife with a clatter, she clasped her arm to her body, feeling the blood soak warm into her shirt, feeling the throb of the injury, weeping with shock and horror and untold relief.

2

She couldn't stay with Karen and Gary any longer. Her social worker told her they were simply too unstable following the death of their son. The state was concerned with the well-being of Mabel Banner, and thought she'd be better off elsewhere.

Mabel didn't want to go. It wasn't that she was terribly attached to Gary or Karen—they were fourth in a string of fosters since she had entered the system—but their house had been home to John, and for that reason alone she wanted to stay. She knew, however, that this mattered little to the state, and so she didn't bother to argue. She sat on the bed in John's room, surrounded by his medals and awards, and tried to say good-bye.

"I hope you're happy wherever you are," she said into the empty air. "I'll always miss you."

Her new mother's name was Gail Thomas, a heavy-set and intimidating woman, and she insisted that Mabel call her *Mom*. The house was shabby and ill-kept, but she had been a foster mother for decades, and was well-trusted by the state. Mabel was one of four children in the house, and the eldest. Gail smiled ingratiatingly to the social worker and spoke in an unctuous voice. Mabel was uneasy, but no one asked her opinion, and so she kept it to herself.

The other children were nine, seven, and four. All girls, by the names of Latisha, Vanessa, and Tabitha. They were sweet and friendly and innocent, and Mabel liked them for that. None of the little girls seemed to feel uncomfortable around Gail, and indeed, she appeared to treat them well in spite of the sparse furnishings and shared beds.

Dinner was macaroni and cheese from the ubiquitous blue boxes, and Gail let Mabel fix it by herself.

"I'm sure you like to be helpful, at your age," she said, and it was not a question or a request, Mabel thought, but a thinly-veiled command. Still, it wasn't that she minded doing it. Gail sat on the front porch in a sagging overstuffed couch and smoked while Mabel drained the pasta and added the butter and milk and powdered cheese. The little girls waited expectantly with bowls at the ready. When it was done and they had eaten, she put the dishes in the sink and rinsed them. Gail came in then, and suggested that she load the dishwasher. Mabel obliged, and the other girls helped her, so it didn't take long. Later that night, she sat on the porch by herself and contemplated her surroundings.

The small clapboard house was one of many rentals that lined the street, most of them in the same state of mild disrepair as it was, with lawns full of crabgrass, weeds and broken toys. Mabel thought back to Karen and Gary's wellkept ranch home, to the upscale middle school she had attended, and a pang struck her heart. Gail came out and sat down heavily next to her.

"I expect a lot, but I hope you won't make a fuss about it," she said. "You seem to be a good girl so far, and I don't want any trouble."

This seemed an unnecessary thing to say, and it was said none too gently. Mabel felt the full impact of the words and could only agree that she wouldn't be any trouble. When had she ever been any trouble? She kept her head down and worked as hard as she could. She was a good girl, her greatest flaw being a deep and abiding cynicism that resided in her heart. She looked at Gail, at her rough hands and stained blouse, and was not comforted. There was something about the woman that was singularly unnerving.

The little girls fought briefly over who Mabel would sleep with, but Gail swiftly put an end to it by matching her up with the youngest, Tabitha. That night, as the smaller girls drifted off to sleep, Mabel lay awake for a long time. She could hear Gail in the living room, watching reality TV and talking on the phone. Snatches of the conversation drifted into the room. *I'm telling you, Marcus, this is the one,* she was saying. *We'll test it out, go slowly, and then build the business from there.* [Something unintelligible.

Then,] *I know, I know. But I have a good feeling about this. She's a pretty one. Looks older than she is, but it shouldn't be a problem.*

Mabel rolled over and shut her eyes. She didn't know what Gail was talking about, but it didn't concern her. If there was one thing she had never been called before, it was *pretty.*

3

Friday night. Mabel came home from school and flung her backpack to the floor. It had been a month since she had arrived at Gail's house, and she felt things were going better than she had expected. She enjoyed the younger girls like she hadn't realized she could, and had already begun to think of them as sisters, especially Latisha, the nine year old. Latisha looked up to her and together they often talked well into the night, sharing their hopes and dreams. They did each other's hair and nails, and although Mabel had never given much thought to her appearance, she had to admit that it was fun to play with the ragged bag of makeup that Latisha had acquired over the years.

The pain in her heart that remained from John's death had begun to ebb, settling into a dull ache instead of the sharp stab that it had been. Although she kept the pocketknife close in her pants pocket always, she rarely took it out anymore, and she had not cut herself in many weeks.

As she flung her backpack to the ground and began to untie her shoes, Gail interrupted her.

"Leave the shoes on, Mabel," she said in her commanding tone. "I've got somewhere to take you tonight. I've got a special job for you to do for me. You don't mind, do you?" Mabel sighed and straightened.

"What is it?" she asked.

"You don't need to know the details right now," Gail snapped. "I'll tell you when we get there."

A neighbor came by to babysit the little girls. Mabel was allowed to eat leftover spaghetti before they departed, although Gail stood over her impatiently until she finished.

"Brush your hair," she ordered, and Mabel brushed it.

"Here's a dress; put it on," she said, and Mabel put it on.

Surely the woman can't expect me to do a real job she thought fleetingly. *There are laws, after all, aren't there?*

The questions remained unasked. The truth was, inside of her heart, she was deeply afraid of Gail, and she knew questions would only aggravate her.

They climbed into Gail's decaying Ford and she revved the sluggish engine into life. Soon, they were headed south through the neighborhood, the houses becoming more and more dilapidated as they went. They turned onto a main street lined with pawn shops and massage parlors, and Gail stopped in front of a small corner grocery store. They got out. Once inside, they were met by a small fidgety man with greasy, slicked back hair.

"Marcus," Gail said, and Mabel's unease ratcheted up another notch. "Here she is. What do you think?"

"Very good," he said curtly, and motioned with his head to a door behind the counter. Gail took Mabel's arm in a vicelike grip and led her through it. As her eyes adjusted to the dark, she saw that the room was lined with curtains, and behind each curtain was a mattress. Dread overtook her, the small hairs on the back of her neck standing at attention, and she struggled to get free of the hand.

"Oh no, dear," Gail said, laughing a short, barking laugh. "This is where you get to pay your way, see? This is how you're going to help Mom out. You're going to be a good girl and do as I say, and everything will be all right. I hate to tell you what might happen if you disobey." Mabel's breath came hard and fast, and she stared at the woman in terror.

"You can't," she said faintly. "They'll find out, the state... the state will find out. You can't–"

"Don't tell me I *can't*," Gail said, giving her a shake that rattled her teeth. "I devoted my life to you brats and you think the state gives a *shit* about you, or me? I'm paid a pittance to put up with you, and I'm telling you that *here* is where I'll get my payback, see? And just because I thought you might protest, I brought something to convince you."

With that, she drew out a syringe and swiftly jabbed it into Mabel's arm. The liquid burned as it entered her body, and she cried out in dismay.

"No, please," she begged as the room began to spin slowly. "Please, don't make me. Don't make me do this." She tried to run but only tripped and fell onto one of the mattresses; her arms and legs were leaden and she was helpless to make them obey her will. Gail smiled an ugly smile and sighed.

"There now," she said. "It will all be over soon, and it won't be so bad after that. We'll go home and you can rest all day tomorrow. You'll see. It'll be just a job after a while."

With that, she was gone, and Mabel was alone, if only for a moment.

Soon she had all the company she never wanted.

4

Mabel worked. She obeyed, and tried not to complain. Gail told her what would happen if she tried to get help. She had warned her of the consequences if she reached out to social worker or guidance counselor or school psychiatrist. "You love those sisters of yours, don't you?" she asked, the day after that first hideous night, when she was still leaking blood and her eyes were red-rimmed and swollen. She nodded, the drugs having worn off enough to allow her to move freely once again. "I know you do. Especially that Latisha; she's a pretty one, isn't she? It would be a shame if you couldn't do your job. It would be a real shame if she had to take your place, wouldn't it?"

Mabel had stared at Gail, dry mouthed. She felt the full weight of her words, and she went numb.

"You can't-" she whispered.

"There you go, with your *you-can'ts* again," Gail spat. "Don't tell me what I can't do, you hear me? You will do as you are told, and those sisters of yours will be fine, you understand? Remember, nobody cares about you, and nobody ever will. You're completely expendable to the state; it'll be your word against mine and you know they'll listen to me before a brat like yourself." She nodded again.

Her days were a blur after that. She went to school during the week and on Friday nights, she worked. Saturdays, she slept. Gail forced her to take the pills she said would keep her from getting pregnant, and she obeyed. The dirty room with the unmade mattresses and the pervasive smell of sweat and bodily fluids became as familiar to her as her own room, and when Latisha and the other girls wondered where she went on Friday nights, she simply told them she was working at a grocery store for Mom.

At Christmas she got an unexpected break. Gail told her she didn't have to work the Friday before Christmas. She sat in the den and played with Tabitha and Vanessa and their dolls. Latisha came in and giggled, twirling her thick black hair as she sat on the battered coffee table. "Guess what?" she said excitedly. "Mom told me I get to work the grocery store tonight. She said you had worked hard enough lately, and so I could take your place. Isn't that great?"

Mabel stared. The words hung in the air, her brain refusing to absorb them and their import.

"What?" she asked faintly.

"The store," Latisha said. "I get to work it tonight. Mom said she'd give me some spending money, too, so I could buy that curling iron I've been wanting; she said–"

"Stay here," Mabel whispered, and rose slowly. She found Gail on the back patio, talking on the phone as usual. When she was finished, she turned to Mabel.

"What do you want?" she demanded, noting the girl's pale face.

"I want to work tonight," she said. "I want to go to work. Don't make Latisha. You said you wouldn't. You said–"

"Don't remind me of what I said, you little bitch," she spat. "I know what I said. But the customers want a fresh face. Don't worry, they still ask for you; you'll still make plenty of money. But Marcus and I know what the market will bear. They want fresh, and they're going to get it, see?"

"I see," Mabel said, and went back inside the house. Walking to the kitchen, she grabbed a towel and twisted it in her hands, thinking. Finally, she returned to the back yard. Gail sat smoking a cigarette and didn't turn when she heard Mabel approaching.

"I told you, no more arguments," she said, taking a long drag. "You weren't really so naïve as to think you were going to be enough forever, were you?"

"I guess not," Mabel said, and drove her pocketknife deep into Gail's neck. The woman let out a shriek, but Mabel muffled it quickly with a kitchen towel stuffed into her mouth. Pulling the knife out with some effort, she drove it in again and again, aiming for the carotid artery, the vessel of grave importance that she had just learned about the previous week in Life Science.

The woman gurgled and flailed, but Mabel's aim was accurate and her passion translated into a pure and perfect strength. It seemed no time at all before Gail slumped onto the patio, a crimson stain spreading quickly across her filthy blouse. Mabel straightened, breathing heavily and stifling sobs, the world red and throbbing, a loud rushing sound in her ears.

She went back into the house and washed her hands and arms. She carefully cleaned the blade of her pocketknife, dried it, and put it back into her shorts pocket. She stripped off her shirt and stuffed it deeply into the trash, crossing the kitchen to go back to her room. She passed the doorway to the den, where the sisters were still engrossed in their play and did not look up. Mabel pulled another shirt from her drawer and threw the rest of her clothes into her backpack. Her mind was a rush of sensations, but it was also strangely clear.

Shouldering the bag, she stepped out the front door, taking great gulps of the thin winter air to calm her racing heart, and looking side to side to see if anyone was around. The street was empty and quiet but for a dog on a chain that barked when it caught sight of her. The sound of the highway could be heard from behind the dilapidated fence that traversed the length of the subdivision.

Mabel ran.

5

Jake Ennis tied the sailboat to the dock and straightened. He needed a drink, badly. The Florida sun was beginning to set, but the heat of it still penetrated his ball cap and made his head throb. It had not been an easy day on the water, and the customers had been demanding and contrary. Still, he had six hundred and sixty dollars cash in his pocket, and that would have to do for now to soften his ragged nerves.

He crossed the dock to the bar and grill perched on the edge of the water, and ordered a whiskey—neat—from Gina, the owner and bartender. Gina was a middle-aged woman with sun-worn wrinkles from a lifetime of living by the sea, but she had been transcendent in her younger days, and the hallmarks of beauty remained in her high cheekbones, clear blue eyes, and thick dark hair.

She and Jake had an understanding. When he needed company at night, he would leave the door to the cabin unlocked, and she would appear. How she always knew, he could not begin to guess. She brought Jake his drink and leaned over the bar, her generous bosom resting on the aging wooden surface.

"Hard day, Jake?" she asked, reading his face with alacrity, as usual.

"Yep," he said, sipping the amber liquid and grimacing. The burn that spread across his chest was comforting, and he relaxed a little, taking his ball cap off and setting it on the bar beside him. He ran his hands through his closecropped and rapidly greying dark hair and sighed. "Lost my first mate again. Not sure why; he just called and said he wasn't coming back. Am I so demanding?"

"No, I'm sure it's not you," she said, her voice soothing.

"Still, I can't seem to keep them," he said. "I'm sure it's the pay; seventy-five dollars a gig isn't much, but I can't very well give more. Do you know anyone who needs a job?"

"Nope," she said. "But I'll keep a sharp eye out."

"Thanks, Gina," he said, draining his drink and motioning for another. "I just don't know what I'm going to do. I can sail *Stella Luna* all right by myself, but I can't play host to customers at the same time very well. And if I can't play host to customers, pretty soon I won't have any, and I'll have to find a real job."

Gina nodded sympathetically and patted his hand.

"I'm sure something will turn up," she said.

He looked around as he sipped his drink and took a few deep breaths, trying to beat down the pessimism that he was feeling. The sun was setting, sending a bright smear of coral across the sky, and as the breeze freshened, the scent of saltwater rose up all around. The palm trees nearby rustled and waved gently above him, and a lizard scuttled across the bar top. He smiled, and felt better in that moment. There was no place more beautiful than Key West, he felt certain, and he was a lucky man to live within its bounds.

Gina finished serving another patron across the room and came back, bringing the mostly-empty bottle of Knob Creek with her and setting it down beside his hat.

"You look like you might just need the rest of it tonight," she said. "Consider it a gift."

"Okay then," he said, gratified. He poured himself another glass and felt happy. Pessimism was not his style, and he didn't like feeling it. Much better to believe the best.

All he needed was someone reliable, someone who could attend to customers' needs while he did the heavy work of sailing; someone who would be satisfied with seventy-five dollars cash in their hand for a few hours work. It was simple enough to teach someone the basics of sailing—he was fairly certain he could teach a moderately intelligent monkey—the human interaction was where he needed help.

He got up, taking his bottle with him, and walked across the wharf to where *Stella Luna* rested. He viewed her with a critical eye, but found little to criticize. She was not a young craft, with dings in her hull and places where a new coat of paint would have served her well, but she was sturdy and fun, a Catalina 35 with just enough room to take out couples and small families who wanted a taste of life on the ocean.

He closed his eyes and breathed deeply. This had always been his dream, after all: to have a charter business that would take him well into retirement. Lila had made him swear that he'd follow that dream, and he didn't intend to abscond on a death-bed promise, if it was in his power to fulfill it. Without a reliable first mate, however, he might have to go back to truly stultifying work—human resources for soulless megacorporations. The thought was unwelcome, and he shuddered in the humid evening air. No, something would turn up. He felt it in his bones, and he took another slug of the whiskey. Something would turn up. It always did.

6

Gina left before daybreak, as was her way, but the memory of her embrace lingered in Jake's mind as he awoke and stretched in his berth. He felt deeply content. Outside the small windows he could hear the birds chirping and the noises of the wharf coming awake. He had slept later than he intended, but his first gig wasn't until 11am and he felt it was going to be a good day. He pulled on his pants as he climbed the steps to the deck, taking stock as he went.

December 29th. The snowbird season was well underway, and his clientele were mostly retired couples who were escaping the frigidity of the northern states for a few months. This afternoon he had several jobs lined up, including an evening sail to watch the sun set. Romantic. He had promised chocolate-covered strawberries and sparkling wine for that one, an extra $50 in his pocket for the luxury. He'd have to go to the store for that. He made a mental note not to forget.

Opening the hatch in the bow of the boat, he checked to make sure his various pool toys and floaties were in good condition. Sometimes people wanted to swim, and sometimes they didn't. You never could tell with these older folks. But he liked to have a few things to make it interesting for them, and the pool noodles and toys were welcome, especially for the older set who tired quickly in the water.

His stomach grumbled loudly and he went below deck once more to shower quickly and change into clean clothes. He studied his reflection in the mirror as he shaved. At fifty-four, his hair was still more pepper than salt, although his beard, when he let it grow, was almost completely grey. Some wrinkles were noticeable, but overall his green eyes were clear and he was often mistaken for a much younger man. Lila had urged him to marry again when she was gone, but he had no interest in such an arrangement. Once had been enough, especially when *till death do us part* had come so unexpectedly quickly to his bride of only eleven years.

Washing the lather from his face, he sighed. Nothing was ever going to fill the hole that Lila's death had left, and he wasn't naïve enough to hope for that. But he was essentially a sanguine man, and he knew that his life was pretty damn good, all in all.

Walking to the bar and grill, he ordered scrambled eggs and cheesy grits and drummed his fingers on the table as he waited. Gina smiled at him as she brought him his plate of food, but neither of them mentioned the night before.

"Hot sauce?" she asked, handing him the bottle.

"You know it," he said.

After he finished, he paid his tab and walked into the parking lot where his battered blue Toyota was parked. He drove to pick up champagne and strawberries, and headed back to the marina. As he parked and got out, a sudden movement in the alley beside the grill caught his eye. At first he thought it was just Gina, emptying the trash, but quickly realized it was someone standing over the bin and picking through it. To his horror, they picked up a wrapper of half-eaten fish and chips and began to devour it.

"Hey!" he shouted, setting his bags on the hood of the car and walking quickly towards the alley. The person looked up from beneath the hood of a grubby sweatshirt, and he could see enough to deduce it was a kid with a dirt-smeared face. Beneath the filth was a look of serious alarm. Grabbing a backpack from the ground, they darted away.

"Wait!" he shouted again, running after them and cursing his knee-jerk reaction.

The kid took a hard left down the boardwalk and tore away from him like a house afire. Jake pursued, but within seconds they had completely disappeared. He stood, hands on his knees, trying to catch his breath.

I gotta start doing some cardio, he thought.

Straightening, he retrieved his grocery bags and went to the bar, where he found Gina polishing glasses.

"Hey Gina," he said. "Have you seen a homeless kid around here?"

"Homeless kid?" she said, a frown furrowing her forehead. No. But I wondered about a box I set in the alley a few nights ago. Looked like somebody had used it for a nest... newspapers all layered inside of it and such. Did you see somebody?"

"Just now," he nodded. "In the alley. Eating somebody's leftovers."

"Ugh," she said, shaking her head. "Wonder what we should do. How old do you think they were?"

"Looked about sixteen, maybe. Hard to say. They had on a hoodie and I didn't get a good look at the face."

"Well, shit. Haven't had any runaway trouble here for a while. Was hoping to keep it that way."

"I know what you mean. Should we call social services?"

"Maybe. Not much to tell them at this point, though."

"True."

They were silent then for a while. Gina poured Barkeeper's Friend on the bar top and began to polish its pitted surface.

"Well, I gotta get ready for my 11o'clock," Jake said finally. "I'll see you later, Gina."

"Later," she nodded.

The rest of the day was spent on the water with various customers, but the image of the kid scarfing down leftovers from the trash bin would not leave Jake's head. He didn't consider himself a sentimental man, but something about the look on the kid's face had gotten to him. Most of the homeless—and all of the runaways—that he had known over the years had a certain hardness about them, a calloused resiliency that kept them going through the rough times. This kid, though... this kid looked... fragile.

He passed out champagne glasses and poured the sparkling wine for the Michigan couple that was celebrating their 50th anniversary with him that evening. Doug and Sharon were talkative and curious, and wanted to know all about *Stella Luna,* so he answered their questions and tried to be jovial, but his heart wasn't in it, and they could tell. Soon they left him alone and sat on the deck, dangling their feet over the side and looking for dolphins while feeding each other chocolate-covered strawberries.

When the sun had set and he was securely moored back at the marina, he thanked the couple for their patronage and pocketed the tip he didn't deserve. He headed for the bar, crowded and bustling for a Thursday evening, as Christmas break was still going strong. Gina was watching for him.

"Got something for you to see," she said, over

the heads of several patrons as she served them their drinks. "Give me a second."

He nodded and stood to the side so as not to be in the way. In five minutes Gina reappeared in the crowd and took him by the hand, leading him through the restaurant kitchen and gesturing for him to look through the window of her office. He obliged. Seated at the desk, devouring a very large cheeseburger and fries, was the kid from the alley.

It was a girl, he saw, the hood off her head and her long blond hair hanging around her shoulders in ragged layers.

The delicate features of her face were clearer now, and a guarded expression had taken over where the vulnerable one had been. As she ate, she seemed to be having a conversation with someone, her lips moving in the empty air between bites.

"I told her we wouldn't call anybody yet," Gina murmured. "Just thought some food would do her good, maybe make her more willing to talk. I haven't gotten much out of her except she says her name is Jane, and that she's eighteen. Not sure if I believe either."

"I see," he said, gazing at the girl and frowning. She could be eighteen, he thought, but it was hard to say. Her face was old and young at the same time. "Who's she talking to? Maybe she's schizophrenic?"

"I don't know. Maybe she's just talking to herself. Anyway, what do you think we should do? I don't wanna call social services if we don't have to."

"If she's an adult, there's not much we can do but point her to the homeless shelter. At least she'd find a decent meal and a shower."

"You sure that's all we can do?" Gina said pointedly. "I mean, I said I'd keep a sharp eye out. Maybe this is the answer to your employment problems."

"What? Hire her as my first mate? Are *you* crazy?"

"I don't see what's so crazy about it. Here's a kid who needs a place to stay, and you've got a place. If she can do the work as well, then your worries are over."

"I wasn't counting on somebody living with me. I'm quite happy on my own, Gina."

"Happy as a clam, I know. But maybe it's not a matter of what *you* need. Maybe it's a chance to do her some good."

"What if she's a drug addict? Lots of kids on the street are. Or a prostitute? Or a felon?"

"Does that look like a felon to you?"

Jack looked through the window again. The girl was done eating, and was sitting, hands folded as though in prayer, eyes closed. She looked like an angel, he thought. "Just go talk to her, that's all I ask. Talk to her. Tell her what you want about the homeless shelter, but be open to other options, huh?" Gina urged.

"Okay, okay," he said, opening the door. At the sound, the girl's eyes popped open and she scrambled to her feet, grabbing the butter knife and looking at him in considerable alarm.

"Hey, it's okay," he said, putting one hand up and moving slowly, as though she were an exotic animal in a cage. He was glad there was no exit door in the office, or she'd have bolted through it in an instant, he was sure. The look of fear covered her face again, and his heart smote him that he was the cause. "I just want to talk, okay?"

She stood still for a moment, and then, with a barely perceptible movement of her head, nodded.

"I'm going to sit," he said, placing himself in the armchair across from the desk. "Won't you?" She remained standing.

"Okay," he said with a shrug. "Suit yourself. I'm Jake Ennis. What's your name?"

The girl stared at him and he felt a growing discomfort. Her brown eyes were large and inscrutable, and he felt like something pinned to a Styrofoam board beneath her gaze. Finally, as he was deciding to get up and leave, she dropped the knife to the table, and spoke.

"Jane."

"Just Jane? No last name?"

"Just Jane."

"Where do you come from, Jane?"

"Oklahoma."

"You're a long way from home."

"Didn't say it was home. Just where I came from."

He laughed. "Fair enough. What brought you to Key West?"

"Cars. Trucks. Sometimes motorcycles."

"So you hitchhiked. That's pretty gutsy. Dangerous, but gutsy."

She shrugged.

"Jane, how old are you?"

A moment's hesitation. Then,

"Eighteen."

"You don't really look eighteen to me. You got any ID?" She shook her head.

"Well, Jane, here's the deal. I don't know if you're really eighteen. I should probably call social services to help you, but I can see by the look on your face that you'd rather me not."

This was an understatement. At the words

social services, her expression changed from guarded to outright terrified. Her eyes darted to the door and back to his face. He spoke quickly.

"I'm *not* going to call social services. But I have a proposition for you. Just hear me out, okay?"

"Can I say no?"

"Of course you can say no, what kind of a question is that?"

She shrugged.

"I have a boat. A sailboat. I do guided tours from the marina here for folks who want to see sunsets and dolphins; crap like that, you know?"

"Sure."

"Well, I need some help. I need a first mate. You ever been on a boat before?"

She shook her head again.

"Doesn't matter. I can teach you easily enough. The sailboat, though; I live on it. You could too."

"Live with you?"

"Yes. I mean, no. Not like that," he said. "I mean, there's plenty of room for two. Two beds. Two *separate* beds, okay?"

She stood, still staring at him in that direct way, and he became acutely aware of the clock on the wall, marking the time with its absurdly loud ticking. The fear on her face was eclipsed somewhat by curiosity, which he took as a good sign.

"Look, I don't know why you should trust me, or why I should trust you, for that matter," he said finally, trying to guess at what was going on in her mind. "Do you do drugs?"

"No."

"Are you a thief?"

"No."

"A felon?"

Her eyes flickered to the ground before coming up again to gaze into his face.

"No."

"Okay. I'm taking you at your word, y'know? And maybe you can take me at mine. I'm no rapist or murderer. I'm just a guy who needs some help on his boat. It's fun work, but hard too. You'd have a place to stay, and some money in your pocket. What do you say?"

"I want to talk to that woman."

"Gina?"

"Yeah."

"Okay," he said, shrugging. He opened the door to find Gina still standing beside it, waiting.

"She says she wants to talk to you."

"Really? All right."

Entering the room, Gina smiled at the girl in a way that she hoped was encouraging.

"You wanted to talk to me?"

"Is he all right?"

"Who? Jake?"

"Yeah, Jake. Is he... all right?"

"If you mean, is he *perfect*, then no," Gina said. "He's got his issues. Wife died a while back, so he's still trying to deal with that. He can be distracted, and distant sometimes. But if you mean, is he *safe*, then yes, he's safe. He's a good man. You'd be hard-pressed to find one better."

"Okay."

"Is that all?"

"Yes."

She left and Jake came back in.

"Any thoughts? I mean, if you need more time to think, that's okay too. I just don't want you running off again."

"I'll do it," she said abruptly. "Okay."

"Great!" he rose and stuck his hand out. Jane stepped back. "Oh hey, sorry; just thought we'd seal the deal with a handshake."

"Oh." She stepped forward again and took his hand in her own. It was small and frail, but the handshake was firm, even powerful. Jake felt strangely elated.

"Lemme just get some food for myself, and we'll go check out *Stella Luna* together; sound good? You can get a shower and clean up."

Her hand went to her hair self-consciously. "Okay."

They sat together in a booth at the bar and grill while Jake ate his chicken fried steak. Noticing her hungry look, he offered her his sweet potato fries, which she made short work of.

"You still hungry?" he asked when he was finished. "How about dessert?"

He ordered the molten chocolate cake and when it came, pushed it across the table to her.

"It's not really my style," he said. "Help yourself."

She devoured it. He liked watching her eat, as he rarely had seen anyone enjoy the simple act so thoroughly.

When she was finished, Jake paid the bill and rose. From the bar, Gina smiled at them and waved.

No more nighttime liaisons he realized with a start. *Ah well... no good deed goes unpunished.*

He sighed.

In the light of the streetlamps that lined the boardwalk, Jane stood, waiting for him to lead the way to her new home.

7

Mabel lay on her bunk in *Stella Luna*, listening to the soft lap of the waves against the hull. She could hear Jake Ennis snoring from his small room and the sound was strangely comforting. She felt safer than she had in months, and with her stomach full and her body clean, she should have been sound asleep long ago. Sleep, however, escaped her.

The trip to Key West had not been without its hiccups. Mishaps, some may have called them, but she preferred to think of them as merely *hiccups*. One beefy truck driver had expected physical payment for his ride from Louisiana into Alabama, but she had pulled out her pocketknife and given him a run for his money. His groping hands would bear the scars for a long time, she hoped. Homeless men and women across the country had shared meals with her and shown her safe places to sleep, and for that she was grateful.

She had started out with no real idea about where to run— only to get as far away from Oklahoma as she possibly could—but when a vagrant in Arkansas had waxed rhapsodic about the warmth of the Florida Keys, a powerful longing to see the ocean had come awake in her heart.

Driving across the water on the Seven Mile Bridge with an elderly couple who had a soft spot for hitchhikers, she felt like she was flying into a vast blue world of untold wonders. A flock of pelicans had risen up next to them, winging their way south, and she had marveled aloud at their prehistoric beauty. The Gulf of Mexico surrounded her, embraced her, she felt, and she thought she might finally be home.

The couple dropped her off at Smather's Beach (the old woman slipping her a twenty before she climbed out of the Volvo), where she stood in awe of the endless sea before her. She had stripped off her shoes and socks and rolled up her cuffs to wade in the water, the clear, warm surf filling her land-locked soul with joy. She bought a meal of tacos from a food truck and felt suffused with peace as the grumbling of her stomach ebbed away. Surely, if luck was to be found, it would be found here.

Being homeless in Key West, however, was a lot like being homeless everywhere else, she found, aside from its warmth and coastal vibe. Safe sleeping spots where you could lie down unbothered by the cops were rare, and already full. She heard from a street performer that there was a shelter with beds, but she avoided it at all costs for fear of social workers finding her there. Instead, she navigated her way to one of the many harbors and sought refuge in the alleys behind storefronts and restaurants. The bar and grill had some excellent leavings, and she parked herself there, thinking she would escape notice if she was careful.

She had been wrong, of course, but now, lying in this bunk, feeling the gentle rock of the boat in the water, she wouldn't say that she was sorry. She was hundreds of miles from Oklahoma and the dead Gail and the cursed room of mattresses, and she would do whatever she had to in order to keep things that way. She lay in the darkness, feeling the comforting weight of her pocketknife in her hand as she slowly opened and closed it. She wouldn't go back, not ever. She would die first.

8

Jake was a patient teacher, and Mabel was a quick learner, which, altogether, made for rapid progress on the boat. He taught her the difference between the mainsail and the jib, the bow and the stern, the rudder from the keel. She learned how to tie the sails down properly, a figure eight knot from a bowline knot, which lines went to what, and to always— always— watch out for the boom. She was surefooted and able as a mule in the Grand Canyon, and not the least bit given to motion sickness, much to Jake's relief.

Their first foray out with customers took place three days after she had come aboard *Stella Luna*, and she fetched refreshments and made conversation like a seasoned cruise director, awkward only when asked about herself. After a few such encounters, Jake had a thought.

"Jane, why don't we just say you're my niece?" he suggested. "It might save you some trouble when it comes to questions about your past."

This she latched onto readily, fabricating a story that became more elaborate with each telling. She was his niece, she said. Her father was Jake's brother John. She was from Miami originally, and had taken a gap year to learn about sailing. She planned to go to college and study marine biology eventually, but for now, she was just having fun. No, she didn't have a boyfriend. No, she didn't want one. She told the story so easily Jake almost believed it himself.

For Mabel, each day was a glorious new adventure. When they were out on the water, nothing could touch her. She felt as free as the fish beneath them, and twice as fortunate. Her first glimpse of dolphins and she was as thrilled as the passengers, her face lighting up and transforming the practiced mask of indifference she usually wore for safety. Jake was charmed by it, and told her so over dinner.

"Shut up," she said, blushing furiously.

"I will not," he answered with a smile. "You're a beautiful girl, Jane. Surely you know that already."

"No," she answered. "I have stringy hair and pale skin and plain brown eyes and no eyebrows. How can I be beautiful?"

"Eyebrows do not dictate beauty," he answered. "And you're taking on more color every day, I might add. You'll be brown as me in no time."

The first thing she did with her earnings was to get her fine hair cut into a pixie, a style that framed her delicate features and gave her even more of a fairy-like appearance than before. Again, Jake was struck by the dichotomy of that face, and marveled that it could look so aged and yet so youthful at once.

She also bought a bikini, a sporty two-piece in a vibrant shade of orange, which she proceeded to wear under her clothes so as to be ready for a dip at any given moment. When they anchored offshore to let the passengers swim, she jumped in with them, demonstrating proper snorkeling style and playing with any youngsters who happened to be along. She was a natural, Jake thought, and blessed the fates that had allowed her to come to him.

9

Mabel awoke with a start.

Someone was calling her name.

"Jake?" From the next room, she heard an unintelligible mumble, the sound of him rolling over in bed, and then silence.

She pushed off the bunk and stood uncertainly in the darkness.

Mabel

The call drifted through the air as clearly as

the sound of crickets that sang to one another in the night. She stepped forward and put her hand on the door, unlocking it and slowly walking up the steps to the deck.

The moon was full and riding high, its face reflected in the shimmering water.

Mabel

The sound seemed to come from all around, and though she searched the darkness for a figure, she could see no one there, neither on the boats beside her nor among the buildings of the marina, looming shadowy and ominous before her.

Her skin prickled and the hairs on the back of her neck stood on end. As far as her eye could see, there were only boats, their masts like so many bare trees stretching up to the sky, and stars that went on forever in the endless black.

Mabel

A sudden thump caused her to spin around, the boat shuddering slightly beneath her. She made her way to the stern, gazing into the dark water below but seeing nothing.

Leaning out, she hung onto the railing, peering down, and caught sight of something large and white rising up through the murk as she stood, transfixed.

The white object broke the surface of the water, and rolled over. With a gasp of horror, Mabel saw that it was a naked body, bloated and grotesque, with long hair that spread out around the head like a dark halo. The arms and legs splayed outward and the belly and breasts bobbed above the rest, face just submerged. Mabel could not find her voice, could not summon her vocal chords to cry out for help, to call for Jake to come. She was paralyzed, watching.

Mabel

The eyes in the swollen face snapped open. With swiftly dawning horror Mabel realized that the thing was Gail, staring at her from beneath the water, a slow smile spreading across the distended features. One turgid hand reached for a rope that dangled from *Stella Luna* and gripped it tightly, pulling. The ship swayed as the corpse began to climb, hand over hand, upward.

Mabel turned to run. Hitting a patch of water on the deck, however, she slipped, fighting to maintain her footing, but fell hard. Something cold and wet gripped her ankle with a fearsome strength, dragging her backwards towards the edge of the sailboat. She grabbed frantically for something to hold onto but there was nothing but the smooth surface of the deck, the nearest cleat just out of reach.

She held the railing as she was pulled halfway off the boat, the thing holding her ankle with all its sodden weight, but just as her strength gave out and she was pulled beneath the surface of the black water, she found her voice.

Mabel screamed.

"Do you want to talk about it?" Jake asked her, over breakfast the next morning.

Mabel shook her head. Talking about it, she suspected, would somehow give it strength to come back again. This, she did not want.

"I never heard anybody scream like that before," he said, impressed. "It's a wonder you didn't wake up the entire marina."

"Didn't I?"

"Nope."

"Good." She shivered even though the air was balmy and the temperature was hovering around seventy-five degrees. Jake looked at her with no small amount of concern as she held her coffee mug with trembling hands.

"Jane..." he started. She looked up at him with her dark and inscrutable eyes. "I'm worried about you."

"I'm fine."

"Are you sure? Are you going to be okay with the customers today, or would you like to sit this one out? You could help Gina around the restaurant, maybe."

Mabel nodded slowly.

"Sit here. I'll go talk to her."

Jake found Gina in her office, and closed the door behind him before sitting down in the tattered leather chair across from her. She looked at him quizzically from over the top of her reading glasses.

"I was wondering if Jane could stay with you today," he said.

"Really? Why?"

"She had a bad dream last night; woke me up with her screaming. Surprised you didn't hear it."

"I always sleep with my sound machine on," she said, setting down the paper she was perusing. "But it sounds like it must have been a doozy."

"She was screaming *No, No* at somebody. Somebody named Gail, or something like that," he said, rubbing his scruff thoughtfully. "Never heard anybody sound so scared. She won't talk about it now, though. Anyway, I thought maybe she could take a break from working for me for a day. Maybe help you out around the kitchen or something."

"She can do that. Or maybe she just needs a day off to knock around town, see a movie maybe. Something a normal kid would do, you know? She can ride my scooter. Maybe she'd like that."

Jake hadn't thought of that, he realized, feeling stupid that he had yet to give his first mate a day of rest.

"That's a good idea. I'll talk to her."

Jane was sitting, staring into the distance, coffee cup empty, her plate of bacon and eggs untouched and congealing before her.

"How about a day off?" Jake asked. "Take some of your hard-earned cash and see a movie, or do some retail therapy for a while. Would you rather do that? Gina says you can borrow her Vespa."

She looked down at her food and was silent. Finally, she sighed and nodded.

"Okay."

"Okay. Are you going to eat, or no?"

"No."

"Let's go then." Jake paid the tab and they walked back to *Stella Luna*. In a moment Mabel had gathered her cash and stuffed it into the pocket of her cargo shorts. Standing on the deck watching Jake take stock of his supplies, she felt suddenly exposed and vulnerable.

"Maybe I shouldn't go. Are you sure you'll be all right?" she asked.

"I'm sure," he said. "We've only got two gigs today. I'll be all right."

"Okay." She said without moving. She felt there were eyes upon her from everywhere, and the urge to dart below deck and stay there forever was strong. Still, she knew this was unreasonable. She stepped onto the dock and walked to the bar and grill, stopping to wave at Jake before disappearing around the corner.

The February day was beautiful and bright, without a cloud in the clear blue sky. As Mabel strapped the helmet on and fired up the engine of Gina's scooter, she felt a surge of wellbeing overtake her previously dark mood. *It was just a nightmare, after all,* she thought. *Just a stupid dream.*

She motored two blocks down and took a right onto Eaton Street, merging carefully with traffic and thrilling at the feel of the wind on her face. John had had a moped, and he had occasionally let her drive it around the block. The scooter was not too different from that, and her memories were all pleasant ones as she drove down the street to Whitehead.

She had no real idea about where she was going, but she had an excellent sense of direction and wasn't worried about getting lost. Taking a left, she passed bars and restaurants, motels and hotels. The sidewalks were crowded with street venders hawking their wares, tourists shopping for souvenirs, and buskers of all kinds performing for loose change.

Rising up before her on her left, she noticed a large Spanish Colonial house with yellow shutters. A sign with the words "Hemingway Home and Museum" caught her eye, and she turned into the parking lot.

Mabel had not had what could be called an excess of education, but she remembered the name *Ernest Hemingway* from her schooling. She parked the scooter and took off the helmet, running her hand through her hair to fluff it. A cat sat at the entrance to the place, eyeing her with some interest. She stooped to pet it, and it wound its way in and out of her legs, mewing loudly. She was charmed.

"He's got six toes on each foot, that one," a voice said from somewhere above her. She looked up to see a man on the upper balcony. He laughed. "Just like the cat Papa loved. Them six-toed cats, they're good luck, so we keep 'em around."

"I see," she said, giving it a final stroke before walking through the doorway. Fishing twelve dollars and fifty cents out of her pocket, she gave the money to the woman stationed at the entrance.

"Thank you, my dear," she said. "I'm afraid the gardens are being prepped for a wedding later tonight, but feel free to look around the museum, and the book store. Would you like a guided tour?"

"Naw," Mabel said. "I'll find my own way."

"All righty then. Just remember, it's a museum, so don't sit on anything that's labeled, okee dokee?"

Mabel wound her way through the house, intrigued by the many small architectural details with their general age and history. On the upstairs balcony she looked out onto the magnificent tropical garden, where masses of people were bustling about, setting up for the previously mentioned wedding.

In the bookstore, she perused the offerings, picking up a biography of Hemingway along with *The Old Man and the Sea* and *A Farewell to Arms*. These she bought, and placed carefully into the paniers on the Vespa. She had missed reading, and thought it would be good for her to have something to do during her off hours rather than stare at the walls and allow her mind to wander down dark channels.

Driving once more down Whitehead, she passed a lighthouse and several churches before coming to a dead end at the Southernmost Point in the Continental United States. Turning northeast, she soon found herself on South Beach, and parked again. Walking with her bare feet in the sand, she felt peace stealing over her once more, the motion of the waves soothing her ragged nerves. She inhaled deeply and closed her eyes, feeling the pull of the current washing the grains out from under the soles of her feet.

Around her, vacationers splashed and yelled and stretched out on blankets and towels, picnicking and tanning, but she stood, a solitary soul, neither vacationer nor resident, and felt the anonymity of her situation. Even Jake, whom she trusted a little more day by day, didn't know her real name, where she had come from... or what she had done.

"Hey," a voice by her elbow said. She turned and saw a tawny-headed, bronzed youth with a Frisbee watching her with azure eyes.

"What?" she said.

"We were just getting a group together to play some volleyball. Do you want to play?" he asked.

"Sure," she said. She hadn't played since her 7th grade PE class, but she thought she remembered the rules. Ten minutes later she was involved in a rousing game, diving to bump the white orb back into the sky for the next person to hit over the net. They played for an hour before switching to Frisbee, which she was not very good at and wound up lobbing into the ocean more often than not. No one seemed to mind, however, and it was always retrieved in good spirit and tossed back to her.

The afternoon was highly enjoyable, and she didn't think of the nightmare or the dead Gail even once. The young man introduced himself as Carl, and he stayed beside her for most of the time. "Want to get some food?" he asked as the day ebbed away. It was getting late, she realized. The sun was touching the water, a brilliant orb of flame in a sky of pink and blue.

"Yeah, okay," she answered. In a moment they were standing at the Cuban food truck, ordering sandwiches and *maduros*. Jane ate ravenously, as usual, and when Carl laughed at her she only stopped long enough to stick out her tongue, which made him laugh harder. As they finished, he walked her back to the Vespa, where she retrieved her helmet and prepared to put it on.

"I really enjoyed meeting you, Jane," he said, standing very close. "Will I see you again?"

"I don't know," she said.

"Do you go to school around here?"

"No..." she hedged. "I'm first mate on *Stella Luna*. It's my uncle's boat. I'm taking a gap year." The practiced lie fell off her lips easily, but never without a pang to her conscience.

"Great," he said. "I go to school at the community college, and other times I'm working over at the Panini joint on Duval. I hope I see you around" She looked into his handsome face and felt a strange sensation in her chest as she struggled to think of something to say, something natural and easy, as though she was just any other girl.

"I hope so too," she finally said. He leaned forward then, and planted a quick kiss on her cheek. Before she could respond, he was trotting away back across the beach and out of sight. She watched him go, wondering at her feelings. Finally, she strapped on the helmet and drove back to the marina, the spot on her cheek tingling all the way.

10

Hemingway, Mabel learned, was a real man's man: a sportsman, a deep sea fisherman, and a big-game hunter. He was married four times and had three sons. He was an ambulance driver and a journalist as well as being a fulltime writer. The black and white photographs she found of him in the middle of the biography fascinated her. She thought him very handsome.

He lived life with a rapacious appetite for adventure, was seriously wounded in WWI, had his heart broken by his nurse in Italy, and survived car crashes as well as plane crashes, brush fires, and pneumonia. In 1954, she was gratified to learn, he was awarded the Nobel Prize in Literature. To Mabel, he seemed like a very bright, hotly burning star, destined to burn out in a spectacular way.

When she got to the end of the biography and learned that he—like his father, sister, and brother— had committed suicide, she found tears rolling down her cheeks, much to Jake's consternation. When he asked if she was all right, she merely pointed to the page and shook her head.

Finished with the biography, she moved on to *The Old Man and the Sea* with great interest, and found the story of Santiago and his battle with the great fish to be keenly poignant, but it wasn't until she dove into *A Farewell to Arms* that she fell truly in love. There, she read:

"The world breaks every one and afterwards many are strong at the broken places. But those that will not break it kills. It kills the very good and the very gentle and the very brave impartially. If you are none of these you can be sure it will kill you too but there will be no special hurry."

She wanted to be one of those broken strong ones very badly, one of those that life sets out to kill in a hurry. She would be brave like that, she thought, taking strength from the words. She felt Hemingway had written them just for her, as though he had seen, from his broad wooden desk, through the decades to her particular situation, and had typed the sentence down for her eyes to see.

She read the passage out loud to Jake and he nodded thoughtfully, saying that he had always enjoyed Hemingway much more than other writers in high school although he could not remember much about what he had written. This, Mabel did not understand. She wept when she finished *A Farewell to Arms* at the sheer, naked pain conveyed in the few words that were used, and marveled once more at the artistic elevation of the simplest themes, of love and fear and courage and disappointment.

The next time Jake gave her the day off, she went straight to the museum and bought three more Hemingway novels. His life in Cuba became of particular interest to her, and when she learned that there was a museum there as well, she begged to go.

"Jake, it's only ninety miles. Can't we get there easily enough?" she asked one day when they were sailing past the condominiums and rental houses with their *SAIL STELLA LUNA* banner draped over the side of the boat, trying to drum up business on a slow Monday afternoon.

"Cuba?" he asked, adjusting the mainsail and tying the line. "You want to go to Cuba?"

"Yes. Badly. You could get us there, couldn't you?"

"In theory, it should be easy enough. Take about fifteen hours, though. And those seas can get pretty rough."

"But you could do it, right?"

"I don't honestly know, Jane. I've never tried it."

"Can we? Please? Pretty please?"

He laughed at her then, and the tattered paperback she held in her hand.

"How many times you read that now?" he

nodded towards the book.

"This one? Three times now. It's my favorite."

"What is it?"

"*For Whom the Bell Tolls*. Listen to this" she said, flipping to a marked page and reading aloud: "*There probably still is God after all, although we have abolished him*. Do you believe in God, Jake?"

"I do," he said after a moment's hesitation. "I have to."

"I've never heard him or seen him do anything for me," she said thoughtfully. "But I suppose he might still be out there, just watching. Maybe just watching and wondering how we will react to the things we go through... maybe if you're especially brave, he'll talk to you."

"I've been brave," Jake said.

"When were you most brave?" she asked.

"Once I was out on the water, by myself, with a storm rolling in. I thought I was a goner for sure; it whipped the waves up over the deck and tilted me so far over I thought we'd go keel-up, but somehow we didn't, and I made it out. I kept my head. That was pretty brave. But I didn't hear God talk."

"Maybe it was just very stupid."

"Sometimes the two are very similar," he agreed. "I've been braver than that, though."

"Really? Tell me."

Jake stood at the wheel then, thinking. She did not interrupt with more questions, but sat on the deck and watched the pastel-colored condos flow past on the shore. She could tell when someone was thinking, and she knew when it was important, somehow.

"I was brave when my wife died. For her," he finally said. "I had to be. She was scared, but I told her there was a God and that she'd go to him and be okay. Maybe that was the most brave I've been."

"Is it brave to believe in God or cowardly?" she wondered aloud.

"I never thought about it. I need to believe in God because I told Lila he was there and I don't want to be a liar."

"Maybe he is always talking," Mabel said. "Maybe we're just not able to hear. It reminds me of this," she flipped to another ticked page and read, *"Because thou art a miracle of deafness; It is not that thou art stupid. Thou art simply deaf. One who is deaf cannot hear music. Neither can he hear the radio. So he might say, never having heard them, that such things do not exist."*

"Yeah, maybe it's like that," Jake said, turning about to head back to the marina. "That Hemingway, he was a pretty smart fellow."

"Yes, he was," she said. "He did everything on his terms." They sailed in silence then for a while, each one lost in thought.

"Hey," Mabel said finally. "What if I learn to sail really, really well, so I can help on the trip across? Would you agree to go then? To Cuba, I mean?"

"Jane," he said. "You need a passport to go to Cuba. Do you have a passport?"

She looked at him then, mouth slightly open, crestfallen.

"We could get one, easily enough," he said. "But there's the small matter of a birth certificate, and your last name, which even I still don't know."

"Right," she said softly. "Right. I hadn't even thought of it. I'm stupid."

"You're hardly stupid," he said. "You were just excited. But how about it... we can get one, right? It will take a couple of months, but it's no problem–"

"No," she said. "I can't."

"But why–"

"Don't ask me why not, please, Jake. Please. I just can't." She clasped the book to her chest, head down, and hoped he wouldn't press it. He was silent for a while, steering and making small adjustments as they coasted along.

"Jane, I'm going to make you a promise," he finally said. "I'll get you to Cuba one day, you wait and see. We'll make it happen somehow."

11

Jake wanted to take a vacation. Business had been good for months, but he was tired. He wanted a break from the demands of customers who thought he ought to be able to conjure dolphins from the waves with a tip of his hat or treated him as though he was part of the package tour. After one trying day in which a bleached-blond retired woman in a thong came on strong to him for the entire three hours they were out, he said he was taking some time off.

"Let's go to the Dry Tortugas," he suggested to Mabel as he lay outstretched on the deck, drinking a beer. "For the weekend. It's not far, and it will be a good chance for you to practice your sailing skills."

"You didn't appreciate Susan's advances?" she teased. He sighed.

"It wasn't like I was disgusted by them or anything," he said. "I'm not made of stone, after all. She just wasn't my type. Like, *at all*. I just wasn't getting through to her, was I?"

"Definitely not," Mabel smiled. "When she said you should meet her for drinks tonight, I thought you might take her up on it, just to shut her up, though."

"If she's as aggressive in bed as she is with the flirting, I would be right to be afraid," he laughed, and then winced. "Okay, that wasn't nice. Let's talk about the Tortugas."

"All right," Mabel said. "How far away are they?"

"About seventy miles to the west. There's a ferry that takes people there in a couple of hours, but it will take us considerably longer if we sail it exclusively. We have to pack all the provisions that we're going to need, because there's nothing once you get there except beauty."

"Have you been before?"

"Several times. But it's been years since the last time. Still, it'll be an adventure for us, right? Just what we need."

"Sounds good to me," she said. "I read that Hemingway liked to fish the Tortugas with his mob of friends back in the 1930s. Let's do it."

They took a couple of days to gather their provisions, loading up *Stella Luna* with coolers full of ice and the fridge with food and bait. Water bottles they bought in bulk from the big box store, trying to predict accurately how much they would need for a week, though they were only planning to stay for the weekend. Weather, Jake said, could be a tricky thing, and they needed to be prepared for the eventuality of not getting back as expected. They planned to fish but took along plenty of protein bars and other dry goods in case nothing was biting (unlikely, Jake said, but you never know).

Jake bought Mabel a fishing pole like his; a seven foot long Penn Squall that looked ready to take on any fish in the Gulf. Mabel posed with it as Hemingway would have; expecting to catch anything the waters could dish out. Jake took her picture and laughed at her and said they weren't equipped to deal with tarpon or marlin, so best to hope for snapper or grouper at the most and leave the rest alone. She thought of Santiago and his battle with the great fish, and vowed to be at least as indomitable if the time came.

"Just don't hook me," he laughed, as she practiced small casts into the harbor while he organized their tackle and found places for all the water bottles that were currently underfoot.

"Maybe I'll catch a shark when we're out," Mabel said, her line stretched between two neighboring sailboats.

"You can catch anything you like except in some places by the islands."

"Why?"

"It's a preserve. Lots of protected spaces, you know?"

"Oh. I get it." Her line suddenly jerked and she sat up. "I think I caught something. Look, Jake. A fishy."

As she reeled in and the line broke the surface of the water, they both laughed as they saw the tiny grunt dangling from the end.

"Dang," she said. "I didn't think anything would go for that big shrimp here in the harbor."

"Here, let me take it off," Jake said, grabbing the line and bringing it in close. He carefully extracted the hook and tossed the fish back into the water, where it slowly disappeared once more.

"Poor thing," Mabel said. "I guess it got a good meal out of the trauma, though."

"Yeah, don't waste any more bait, huh?" Jake said, patting her on the back. "We're going to need that before the trip is over."

"Right." She reeled in the rest of the line and set the pole in the hold with Jake's. "What can I do to help?" she asked.

"Go through the first-aid kit," he said, pointing. "Make sure we've got everything we need."

"Aye aye, captain," she said, saluting smartly with a smile on her face. "When will we set sail tomorrow?"

"I want to get an early start. What do you say to six thirty?"

"Sounds good to me."

The next morning Mabel was awoken by Jake rummaging around for his clothes, and she sat up, stretching. A thrum of excitement was flowing through her at the prospect of the journey, and she dressed hurriedly and splashed her face with water in the tiny washroom.

Once on deck, she untied the lines and wound them around the cleats, and Jake motored *Stella Luna* out of the harbor and into the Gulf.

The May morning was beautifully clear, with the temps in the mid-eighties already, but the breeze that ruffled Mabel's hair was fresh and cool. She breathed deeply, and marveled anew at her good fortune. Here she was, with a good man who treated her well and expected nothing but hard work in return, living life on the cerulean sea. If the bad dreams that plagued her nights would only dry up, things would be perfect.

She had ceased looking over her shoulder for the authorities many weeks before. Social services did not haunt her thoughts anymore, and she told herself that any cops in Oklahoma who might want to connect her with the death of Gail must surely have given up. The niggling idea that she ought to tell Jake the truth about her life (and her name) never left her, though, and she stuffed it down, telling herself that she would, when the time was right.

The Gulf seas were gentle in the bright morning light, and Jake and Mabel unfurled the mainsail and pulled it aloft. It luffed gently in the breeze and Jake angled it to better catch the wind until they were heading due west at a fair clip.

Once all sight of land faded into the distance and the sails were billowing strongly, Mabel got out the rod and reel again and cast hard into the sea.

"You'll probably not catch anything that way, with us going full-bore like this," Jake said with a smile.

"I know," she said, shrugging. "I just want to practice."

She found the monotony of casting out and reeling in incredibly soothing, and as she sat on the deck with her feet dangling over the side, feeling the spray of the water on her face, she didn't think there could possibly be anything better. "I want to catch a Marlin," she said. "Like Hemingway. Like Santiago. A big fish with a fin. How hard would that be?"

"Incredibly hard," Jake said, laughing. "You need quite a bit of muscle to get one of those bad boys into a boat, and the deep sea fishing boats have special chairs to sit in while you wrestle the thing. You've noticed them in the harbor, right? Those boats with special chairs that help you brace the pole and stuff?"

"Yeah."

"You'll need to have the right bait first, though. A Marlin's not going to go for shrimp or something puny like that. You need bait fish for them. And heavy duty fishing line. Usually a deep sea fishing boat has several lines going at once to maximize their chances of hitting a Marlin, and when they do, it takes a full grown man all his strength to bring it in."

"You don't think I could do it?" Mabel said, flexing her wiry bicep.

"Well, I wouldn't say you *couldn't*..." he hedged. She smiled. "But I would be mighty surprised."

Suddenly, Mabel's line went taut, and the pole was very nearly jerked out of her hands.

"Shit!" she exclaimed.

"Hang on tight," Jake urged. "You've got something big!"

"I'm hanging on," she said, her heart racing in her chest as the line buzzed and spun. "What should I do?"

"Pull it in!"

She grabbed the handle of the reel and began to turn it backwards but the best she could do was just keep more from spinning out. She could hardly believe the pressure against her fingers as she gripped the pole and braced it under her arm for more control.

"I can't believe you caught something just messing around!" Jake said, laughing.

"What is it?"

"I don't know yet. Could be a shark. Could be a tuna. We'll have to see. Don't lose it!"

"I'm trying my best," she grunted, reeling in ever so slightly. Inch by inch the line was wound back into the tackle, and the pole bent low.

"It won't break, will it?" she asked.

"Hard to say," Jake answered. "We only bought thirty pound line. If it's bigger than that it very well might break it."

Suddenly there was a commotion in the water and a vibrantly-colored fish broke the surface, thrashing. Mabel reeled hard and gained several feet.

"It's mahi mahi," Jake said. "Looks at least twenty pounds I'd say. Amazing!"

Mabel didn't know mahi mahi from tuna, but she knew that she was looking at the most wildly beautiful thing she had ever seen. The fish was a rainbow of color as it fought her hook, and as its strength flagged, she brought it close to the boat, marveling.

"It's so gorgeous!" she said as Jake put on gloves and pulled the fish onto the deck. The creature gasped and flopped, the iridescent scales rippling.

"It's too big for us to keep," Jake said. "But I want to get a picture of you with it, at least. Stay here and hold it still while I get my camera."

Mabel obeyed, kneeling on the fish's side, stroking it and speaking in what she hoped were reassuring tones while holding firmly onto the line that stretched from its mouth. In moments Jake emerged from the cabin with his camera in his hand.

"Smile!" he said, and Mabel smiled, heart still pounding from excitement and exertion. Jake took several pictures and then came close to extract the hook. Moments later, the big fish had splashed back into the water and disappeared from sight. Jake knelt on the deck, looking at Mabel with admiration.

"Well; we didn't expect that to happen, did we?" he said. "It's too bad we couldn't have kept it; mahi mahi is delicious fried in butter."

"I couldn't have eaten anything that pretty," said Mabel. "I need to catch some ugly fish." Jake laughed.

"Well, don't count on too much that's ugly! Most of the fish here in the gulf have their own kind of beauty. We've got to keep some of them, though, or we'll get awfully hungry for real food. There's only so many power bars and bologna sandwiches I can stand."

"Okay," she said. "I'll try to get over it."

Jake went back to sailing, correcting their course slightly while whistling an aimless tune. He turned on the radio and the sounds of the alternative rock station filled the air, between the weather reports put out by the naval base. Mabel went back to casting and sat, staring out at the endless water around her. She hoped the fish was not too frightened and would recover nicely.

She caught nothing more until the Marquesas Islands came into sight. There, Jake said, the reef would provide excellent prospects for fish the size of which they were looking for. They pulled in the sails and floated in some of the clearest water Mabel had ever seen, the reef off the port bow visible beneath the gentle waves that lapped at the boat.

"Now, let's see what we can get for dinner," Jake said, threading a hook through a meaty shrimp and casting out. Mabel followed suit and they sat in silence for a while, expectant.

Sailboats and yachts dotted the water around them, and they could hear the shrieks of swimmers and snorkelers carried to them over the waves.

"Are they going to scare the fish away?" Mabel asked.

"Hopefully they'll scare them towards us."

Mabel was hot now, the sun being well overhead and temperatures soaring into the nineties. The breeze came and went, but the water beckoned alluringly. Mabel stripped off her shirt and sat in her bikini, enjoying the feel of the sun on her skin. She was very brown now, as Jake had told her she'd be, and she lifted her face to the sky with a sigh of contentment.

"Can I jump in?" she asked.

"Sure. Just don't get in the way of my line."

She reeled in, set aside the rod, let the ladder down, and plunged in. With a shout of relief, she came up, shaking the water from her eyes.

"Jake, come in!" she said. "It's so wonderful."

"Maybe later," he said, reeling in for the twentieth time, checking his lure, and casting out again. "If nothing hits my hook we're going to be having bait for dinner."

As if on cue, however, the line went rigid and the rod bowed. He whooped and pulled hard, reeling in as he did so. Soon he was hauling a ten pound grouper out of the water, and Mabel clambered back aboard to see it.

"Hey, that's what I'm talking about," she said. "Ugly."

"What do you mean?" Jake retorted. "Look at those lovely speckles and spots. It's a beautiful fish too."

"Maybe to another grouper. Not to me," she shook her head.

Jake pulled out his fillet knife and a pair of pliers and set about filleting the fish, which Mabel watched with some fascination. Working one side of the fish and then the other, it took him no time at all to get the meat off, removing even the meat from the fish's throat and cheeks, where Mabel would never have even thought to look. When he was done, he heaved the carcass back into the water and put the fillets and meat in the cooler.

"Handy skill, that," she remarked admiringly. "Can you teach me?"

"I can teach you anything," he said. "Really you just have to have a sharp knife and some confidence. You can't be timid. Can you do that?"

"Sure."

"I'll let you do the next fish, how about that?"

"Great!"

Mabel sat down once more to fish, determined to be patient. She stuck her hook firmly into a sardine and cast out. Within moments she had a fish, and as she pulled it onto the boat, Jake nodded approvingly.

"Yellowtail snapper," he said. "A nice one, too! That will be tasty. Ugly enough for you?"

"No!" she exclaimed with a laugh. "That fish is beautiful! Look at its lovely tail! But I'll eat it anyway." The afternoon's fishing and swimming had made her fiercely hungry, and the thought of a fish dinner made her mouth water.

"Ok then," he said, and took the hook out of its mouth. With his tutelage, she soon had it filleted, albeit crudely, and put in the cooler alongside the grouper.

"Good job," he told her. "You're definitely not timid with a knife."

"Thanks," she said, blushing faintly.

"That's a good day's fishing for two," Jake said, and he brought out a beer. Mabel took a bottle of water and together they toasted the day. The sun was lower in the sky, the time around 3pm, and Jake set about frying up the grouper, along with some squash they had brought with them. By the time it was done Mabel was properly ravenous, and devoured the meal with her characteristic speed. Jake laughed and shook his head.

"Are you sure you even tasted it, Jane?" he asked.

"Sure I did. It was delicious," she said.

"You remind me of a pelican. All right. Well, let's press on, shall we?"

Hoisting the mainsail once more, they set off to the west. The Dry Tortugas were only fifty more miles, and the trip was pleasant and mostly easy, with five foot seas to keep it interesting. As the sun touched the ocean, the low lying islands were on the horizon. Jake maneuvered around Garden Key to the boat pier and secured *Stella Luna* there. "Shall we get out and walk around the fort?" Jake asked. "I have to go get us a boat permit anyway. Do you want to come?"

"Of course," she said, pulling on her clothes over her bathing suit. They stepped onto the pier and Mabel took in the sight of the 170-year-old fort and felt a chill up her spine. History was thick in the air, and she could almost hear the voices of the people, long gone, who had built and defended it, lived there and died there. With the sun rapidly setting, it cast long shadows out over the water and looked thoroughly haunted.

She and Jake walked through the doors into a large, open courtyard where people milled about, talking and laughing and taking pictures, and this alone kept Mabel's mind from straying down dark passages for too long. Still, the shadows that stretched over the grass were ominous, and she wished she had stayed on the boat.

Jake, seeing her anxious face, asked her what was wrong.

"I don't know," she said. "It's just... if there were such things as ghosts, they would live here. For sure."

"I see," he said, nodding but obviously not sharing her sense of the macabre. "Well, let's get that permit and get back to the boat, okay? Then we'll find a good anchorage and eat some dinner. You'll probably feel better then."

Mabel nodded. At the visitor's center, Jake got the permit and grabbed a brochure. Following Mabel back to *Stella Luna* at a brisk pace, he called out facts to her as they went. "Hey, did you know it took some sixteen million bricks to build this thing? And that it had 420 guns when it was built? At its height nearly 2,000 people lived here, including some women and children. Hey! Jane, are you listening?"

Mabel was not listening. Mabel was climbing back aboard the boat and untying it from the pier. Jake stepped onto the deck and helped her, winding the line around his arm and securing it before motoring back around the key to the anchorage. With the anchor down and the sails wrapped, Mabel sat with her back to the fort, looking out instead at the increasingly dark sky, musing.

"What's on your mind?" Jake asked, cooking the rest of the grouper and setting it in front of her. She picked at it listlessly and the lines on his forehead became more pronounced. "Are you okay?"

"I just don't like the fort," she said. "It makes me... nervous."

"I'm sorry," he said. "I thought it was kind of cool. Maybe it will look less imposing tomorrow morning in the bright light of day, huh?"

"Probably," she said, trying to cheer up and eat. The fish was wonderful, tasting of butter and herbs, and the potatoes were fried to perfection. Still, she ate slowly for once, and tried to understand the feeling of doom that had overtaken her. "I'm sure I'm just being silly."

"Not silly," Jake shook his head. "Some people are just extra sensitive to supernatural stuff. Maybe you're one of them."

That night she dreamt that she was standing on the top of the fort's wall, looking down upon the water beneath a bright waxing moon. *Stella Luna* bobbed below her along with several other boats of varying sizes, and she knew, somehow, that she was safely asleep in her berth, and yet standing atop the wall at the same time. She didn't want to be on the wall; she wanted to be reunited with her body, to be sleeping as soundly as Jake, who never dreamt of anything but Gina.

She turned to find her way off the fortress, to find the stairs and to make it back to the boat, even if she had to swim through the dark water to get there, but as she turned she saw the figure she dreaded most standing some hundred feet away, monolithic in the moonlight, just standing and staring.

Gail. Dead, of course, her face rotting and jaw hanging open, held to her skull crookedly by one membranous tendon. Mabel froze, willing herself to turn and run the other way but she was incapable of movement, and could only whimper, blood rushing in her ears, heart thudding in her chest.

Mabel came the familiar call, just as she expected it would.

You killed me, Mabel. You killed me dead. And now I'm going to do the same to you. I'm going to kill you and throw you to the sharks but you won't be dead, no, you'll be a ghost like me, forever doomed to walk these walls and visit people in their dreams

The apparition moved towards her, staggering on its bent and decaying limbs, but coming closer just the same. She turned to run but as she did she felt the powerful grip take hold of her, the frigid, bony hand, this time around her neck, lifting her off her feet and dangling her over the low battlement of the wall, where nothing but rocks lay below. She tried to scream but her air was cut off, and then she was falling towards the rocks and water, just falling and falling into a dark void of nothingness and terror.

She awoke, gasping and crying. Jake stood over her, chafing her hands and repeating words of comfort.

"It's okay, Jane," he said softly as her eyes fixed upon his wonderfully real and sane face that never looked upon her with anything but tenderness and affection. "It's okay."

She sat upright and wrapped her arms around his neck, sobbing into his shoulder as he patted her back and kept on talking in low, soothing tones. As her cries ebbed away, she lay back down and he offered her a drink of water. She took it gratefully.

"Now, do you think you can go back to sleep?" he asked.

"I don't want to," she answered.

"Understood. Do you want to talk about it?"

"No."

"Okay. Do you want me to sit up with you?"

"Yes."

Jake yawned, pulled on a shirt, and set about making some coffee. The time was just after 4am, and as he spoke, he told Mabel stories from his youth in the boondocks of Georgia, which caused her to laugh and were altogether a great distraction from her dreadful and disturbing dream.

They stood out on the deck and watched the sun creep slowly over the eastern horizon, ignoring completely the fort behind them to the west. Finally, when the world was full of light and beauty once more, Mabel felt she had the strength to turn and look at the fort, which was, as predicted, perfectly unassuming in the bright daylight.

She stood with her mug of steaming coffee and felt her equilibrium return. She had dreamt of Gail again, just as she had suspected she would, yet here she was, still alive and healthy and with all faculties intact. Gail was dead and gone and if the worst she could do was inhabit the place between wakefulness and sleep, then there was nothing she could really— not *really*—do to her at all.

"Hi neighbors," said a voice off to the left. They turned and nodded at the young, bearded man who stood on the deck of his Presto 30 just fifty feet away. He too held a mug of coffee and appeared to be greeting the sunrise. "Y'all having a good trip?"

"Sure are," Jake answered. "And you?"

The man's handsome face wrinkled into a broad smile.

"Wife divorced me. I'm loving being single. Name's Dan. And y'all are?"

"Jake and Jane," Jake said. "Sorry about the divorce."

Dan continued to grin. "Bought this boat with the money I've saved now that she's gone. It's the life, I tell you. I'm new to sailing, but all things considered, it's going really well. I've been here for three days; going to leave tomorrow."

"Well, be careful out there," Jake said. "I think I heard that things are going to get rough in the next couple of days. We were going to head back tomorrow too, but we may have to wait it out instead."

"All right," the man said. "I'll be careful. Y'all have a nice trip, now. Enjoy each other." He winked in an exaggerated fashion, and headed below deck. Mabel recoiled somewhat and looked at Jake. His brow was furrowed.

"He didn't think–?"

"I think he did think."

"Huh."

There didn't seem to be much to say past that, so they finished their coffee and ate the Danishes that Jake heated up in the tiny oven.

"Hey, did you know that Hemingway got marooned at Fort Jefferson for seventeen days on one of his trips with his group? They meant to only stay a week but bad weather trapped them."

"I did not know that," Jake said. "You're a veritable font of Hemingway information, aren't you?"

"They had enough liquor and coffee for the whole time."

"No doubt."

"But they had to fish for food after the first week."

"No power bars back then," Jake said.

"Nope."

"Let's snorkel, shall we?" Jake asked. Mabel nodded enthusiastically, and Jake prepared the boat to head to the west side of the island, a prime snorkeling area. In moments they had donned their bathing suits and were in the warm, inviting water, where they gloried in the sight of turtles and parrotfish, dozens of smaller, brightly colored tropical fish, and even one large, slowly moving reef shark.

When they had thoroughly examined the region, they swam back to the boat and climbed aboard, Mabel feeling lighthearted and unworried once more. Jake prepared the yellowtail for lunch, and she didn't think she'd ever tasted anything better.

"You say that every time you eat anything," Jake laughed, poking her in the ribs.

"I enjoy food; so sue me," she said.

"I enjoy you enjoying it. I just wonder if it'll ever put any meat on your bones. Maybe you need to chew more carefully," he suggested. She smiled, and they finished their meal off with some gourmet chocolate chip cookies Jake had picked up at the specialty grocery store. Mabel wiped her mouth and sighed contentedly.

"Now what?" she asked.

"Now, we fish some more. We need more dinners, after all, unless you want to live off the power bars, which I definitely do not. What do you say?"

"Can't wait!"

They tacked around the island again, sailing out to where fishing was permitted, and baited their hooks. Casting them into the water, they waited. Mabel noticed the Presto 30 sailing to the east and pointed it out to Jake.

"Dan is probably headed home, but I wouldn't do it if I were him. He ought to wait out the weather that's coming, like we're going to. The Gulf can get pretty dicey for a beginner, especially."

They caught several small grouper and a nice yellowtail and filleted them, putting them on ice. Jake listened to the radio for a while and confirmed that there was a storm brewing. He pointed out the thunderheads in the distant east, and shook his head.

"Hope Dan does all right," he said.

The next two days were full of exploring the various reefs and fishing until their bait was almost gone. Mabel and Jake played Yahtzee and talked until deep into the night about anything and everything. Everything, that is, except Mabel's past. Sometimes the breaks in the conversation would stretch out in the empty air, and Mabel would feel the truth upon her lips, just waiting there to be spoken aloud, but she always snatched it back before it could fall, irretrievable and life-altering, into Jake's ear.

If she told Jake the truth, nothing would be the same, of this she was certain. He would have to call the authorities, and at the very least, she'd have to go to trial, go back to Oklahoma, a place she considered forever accursed. And what then? Prison?

Maybe she'd be found not guilty, an idea she found unlikely. After all, she had murdered Gail in cold blood; stabbing her in the throat as she smoked a cigarette on the back porch. No jury would find her innocent. But even if they did, so what? More foster homes, more uncertainty. She'd lose this magnificent freedom, this marvelous bit of paradise that she had found with Jake under the vast ocean reflecting sky. No. She would remain *Jane Ennis* for as long as she possibly could, for as long as it was up to her.

Jake, for his part, never pushed for the truth of her past, though he did wonder. It entered his mind that perhaps she wasn't eighteen at all; perhaps she was younger, and she should be in school. This thought burrowed into his subconscious and niggled occasionally. That she was smart was no question; she was wicked smart, and strong, and fierce, and he thought she deserved the very best that life could offer.

Maybe that was this: a life on the ocean as his first mate. She certainly seemed to enjoy it. But she was so very young. What of her next steps? What future did she have? She had no opportunity to ever have her own place, her own love, her own family. She had no insurance, no retirement plan. She met no one new and didn't seem to want to. It was very apparent that she was running from something, but what?

What could someone so young be running from? How long before it caught up to her? And how would he be implicated in the drama?

One day, he told himself, everything was certain to change, for that was the way life was. Fluid. For now, however, he was going to live in the moment with her, enjoying the pleasures of the Gulf and the Florida Keys as thoroughly as possible. And if the past ever came knocking, he would bar and lock the door if necessary to keep her safe.

12

On the third day of their vacation, Jake set the sails and pointed the vessel back to the east. The weather had cleared once more and all looked well for their passage across the Gulf. Some contrary wind was blowing, but with Jake's skills, it was hardly any trouble at all to make it work for them instead of against them. He showed Mabel the finer points of sailing a zig zag pattern, close hauled beside the wind so that they still moved forward.

Halfway to the Marquesas Islands, a ship appeared off their port bow, a form on its deck waving frantically. Jack and Mabel both realized with some dismay that they recognized it.

The Presto 30 had been beaten and bruised, its mast completely broken, the sails hanging uselessly. The entire ship was listing hard to starboard, and at the helm they could see the form of Dan, bailing buckets of water out from below deck and waving at the same time. Jake honked the horn and sailed towards the disabled craft.

"Guess you found the bad weather," Jake exclaimed, pulling up carefully and slowly along the port side of the Presto.

"I guess so," Dan said, and he wasn't smiling anymore. "I hit some really scary stuff, man, and I thought maybe I'd capsize. Broke my mast and I fouled my prop with something. I can't get it to start. And my phone got wet so I couldn't call for help. I should have listened to you."

"I'm sorry to see your boat in such rough shape," Jake said. "But it's nothing a little money can't fix. Here, let's see if we can't get you some help from the coast guard, eh?"

Jake pulled out his phone and stood, finger poised over the button to call.

"Okay. Thanks, man. Jake, wasn't it? And Jane?" Jake nodded.

Dan tipped his cap to Mabel, but Mabel stared, a growing sense of dread in the pit of her stomach. Something was not right, though she couldn't for the life of her put her finger on it.

Jake had the phone to his ear, listening to it ring, while Dan reached out his hand to the lifeline and pulled hard. In an instant he had stepped onto the deck of Stella Luna, and just as quickly, pulled a gun out of the back of his pants.

Raising the weapon, he squeezed off a quick succession of shots before Mabel could think to move: two straight into their radio, and one into Jake. He crumpled to the deck, his phone skittering into the water. Mabel screamed and lunged towards him but Dan intercepted her, grabbing her tightly in his arms and pointing the gun at her midsection as she struggled.

"Shh, shh, shh," he hissed into her ear. "Quiet, or you'll get a bullet in your belly and a very nasty, prolonged death."

She quieted herself then, and became very still,

mind racing. She could feel the familiar weight of her knife against her leg, and she slipped her hand in her pocket to get it. Before she could do anything else, however, Dan spun her around to face him.

"I need something off that stupid boat before I take yours, okay? And you're going to go over there and get it for me, or your friend there is going to get another bullet, and this one straight into his brain, got it?"

She nodded, eyes wide and breathing hard.

"It's a duffel bag, okay? You'll know it when you see it. Now get over there and get it. I'll wait. No funny business."

Nimbly crossing to the other boat, Mabel went into the flooded cockpit and located the duffel. While in the depths of the Presto, she took out her pocket knife and opened it, slipping it back into her pocket swiftly. Lifting the sodden duffel in her arms, she carried it to *Stella Luna*. Dan snatched it from her and threw it below deck, pointing the gun at all times at her head. From the deck, Jake moaned and tried to get up.

"Stay where you are if you know what's good for you, you hear?" Dan shouted at him. He became still again, and Dan turned back to Mabel.

"You're mighty pretty," he muttered. "And I haven't gotten any in a very long time; not since the wife left me, you know? So I'll be taking a happy little memory with me before I toss you two overboard."

"No," Mabel said in a small voice. "No, please."

"Please, huh? Such pretty manners."

Dan moved closer, slowly backing her into the cockpit. In moments she was pinned to her berth, his breath hot on her cheek. The button on her shorts gave him trouble, and he wrested it off with a violent tug, but when he released her for a moment to unzip his cargo shorts, she lunged up, pocketknife flashing, and carved a wide slash across his face. Blood poured from the wound and he cried aloud, stumbling backwards, rage and surprise overtaking his features.

The gun fired once, then twice, and Mabel felt her thigh burn fiercely, but the air once again blazed red before her eyes and she ran forward, stabbing with the knife until it was slick with blood. Dan stumbled backwards and up the steps, shooting blindly. Bullets flew past her ears and lodged in the woodwork behind her, but still she pressed forward until the man was stumbling up the stairs and across the deck, where she aimed one last slash at his throat as he toppled over the lifeline and into the water.

Running to the cockpit, she fired up the engine and put the boat in gear, shooting away from the disabled Presto and the doomed man who was even at that moment screaming epithets into the space between them.

Panting, she stepped over the lines to reach Jake. The air cleared of its red haze and she could see plainly that he was in desperate shape.

There was a hole in his shoulder and it was bleeding freely. She stripped off her tank top and pressed it to the wound, running back to the first aid kit to find ace bandages, which she wound around his shoulder tightly, holding the top, which was rapidly turning from white to bright red, in place.

She examined her own injured leg and winced. The bullet had grazed her thigh, the blood soaking her shorts and running down her leg, but she could see that the laceration was superficial and was even now drying up.

"Jake? Jake, can you hear me?" she spoke to

him, patting his cheek gently with one bloodied hand, and he stirred.

"Jane? What happened?"

"He shot you. Dan. He tried to kill us, but we got away. We got away, Jake. Don't worry. We'll be all right; just have to get back to Key West."

"Jane," he said. "Jane." And he was out again. Mabel fought tears, but as she nearly gave in to her grief, the engine coughed, sputtered, choked and died. Getting up, she crossed to the cockpit and tried to turn it on again. No luck.

"Dammit! Dammit, dammit, dammit!" she kicked the wall, crying out in pain as she did so.

She reached for the radio, but even as she did so she knew it would not work. Bullets had completely obliterated its panel, as well as the navigation, and as she spoke into the receiver, nothing but dead air met her voice. She wept then, in frustration and fear, sweeping the horizon with her gaze in hopes of seeing another ship, but there was nothing but endless blue ocean.

Looking up at the billowing sails, she felt hope revive briefly, but as she surveyed the destroyed navigation panel, a sense of doom overtook her. Without navigation, she would have no way to get back safely to Key West.

Dear God, she prayed in desperation. *If you're there, send help.*

13

Mabel was tired, and getting steadily more so. Her leg ached, and she tightened the bandage around it. She made Jake drink some water but he was growing noticeably weaker. The sun set, and with it went any of Jane's ability to sail east with any certainty.

"Jane," Jake said faintly. "Jane, don't forget to wing the jib. We'll lose power if you over trim..."

"Don't worry, Jake," she answered in what she hoped was a soothing tone. "I've got it taken care of."

"Jane," he said again.

"Yes?"

No answer. She lay down next to him, placing a towel under his head to cushion it against the fiberglass.

"Please be okay, Jake. Please don't leave me here alone."

His shoulder was sticky with drying blood, but the wound seemed to have stopped actively bleeding. She stared up at the stars blazing in their respective places in the ebony sky, comforting her heart with their constancy. Another hour passed and she dozed off several times, waking with a jolt and increasing despair. The clock read 2:37am and she ate a power bar to keep up her strength, though it did nothing to make her feel powerful. She felt thoroughly drained, deeply weak, and increasingly frightened.

Several boats had passed close enough to see her, but though she screamed until she was hoarse and waved her arms frantically, none of them had noticed her plight.

She sat beside Jake and rubbed her eyes, sighing heavily. Crossing to the cockpit, she tried the engine again but it made no noise at all, not even turning over once.

Sudden movement off the port bow caused her to startle, and as she turned, she cried out in abject terror.

A figure was approaching her, illuminated by the moon and striding over the waves as naturally as if walking through an open field. She stared, hand over her mouth, heart pounding wildly in her chest.

The person was male and heavy-set, dressed in khakis, a button down shirt, and a pith helmet. His good-natured face was bearded in white and neatly trimmed. As he walked confidently over the waves, he sent up a spray of water with his boots. A rifle was slung over his shoulder, and as he approached, one name alone sprang to Mabel's mind.

"Hemingway?"

He drew closer, looking stern.

"Mabel," he said, stepping into the boat on an accommodating swell of water. "What do you think you are doing out here?"

"I'm stuck, Papa," she said, the nickname falling easily from her lips. "Jake's hurt, and the navigation is wrecked. I need to get home, and fast."

"Is that so?" he said, frowning.

"Yes; Jake is hurt and I need to get back to Key West," she repeated. "Only I can't tell which way is east now that the sun's gone down. I have no way to tell."

"I see," he said. "Can you get up? You are injured as well."

"I can, Papa. It's just a flesh wound."

"You are very brave, Mabel. But you are tired. That's why I've come to you."

Hemingway sat down beside Mabel and unslung the gun, laying it carefully on the deck. He stretched, and rubbed his hands together.

"Have you got anything to eat?"

"Power bars," she said, gesturing towards the kitchen. "And fish, if you want to cook it."

"I do indeed," he said, getting up to rummage through the cooler. Pulling the snapper from its depths, he retrieved a pan from the cupboard and put it over the heat of a burner on the stovetop. He added the fish and some seasonings, and tossed them all in oil. In twenty minutes he was done, and the smell wafting through the air made Mabel's mouth water, reviving her dull senses. He passed her a plate.

"Take it," he ordered. "You need strength."

Gratefully, she consumed the fish, and more than just filling her belly, it awoke her mind and sharpened it. She took a long drink of cold water and felt she might make it after all.

"Papa," she said. Hemingway looked at her, bushy eyebrows raised. "Thank you."

"For what?"

"For writing your books. And for coming to me."

"You're very welcome."

"I do wish you had not killed yourself, though."

"We wish a great many things, don't we?"

"We do."

"But now we need to work, and work quickly. Your friend will need a great deal of help once he gets to civilization," Hemingway said. He moved nimbly for a big man, and soon he had the sails trimmed and their course adjusted.

Suddenly the wind filled the mainsail, and they were moving with purpose. Mabel's heart leapt with excitement to feel the jolt of the hull as it bounced through the water, and the spray on her face felt like life itself.

"We're going to make it!" she said excitedly. Hemingway merely nodded and moved to the wheel to adjust the direction.

~~~

They sailed on eastward, talking about his works, discussing the themes of death and grief and strength, and Mabel did not grow tired again. As the first twinkling lights of Key West appeared on the horizon, she turned to ask him a question about God and the afterlife, thinking that, if anyone would have answers, it would be him.

He was gone. She was as alone as before, with only the sound of the waves and the rustle of the sails to meet her call.

Checking on Jake, she found him feverish and breathing shallowly.

"Are we home yet?" he whispered.

"Almost," she said. "I can see the lights."

"You did it, Jane," he said, the trace of a smile flickering over his pale face. "You did it."

"Yes," she said, as he closed his eyes and drifted off again. "We did."

14

When Mabel pounded on Gina's door at 4:30 am to ask her to come quickly and call an ambulance, Gina responded instantly and decisively. She and Mabel drove Jake's car to the hospital and waited less-than-patiently in the small ER family room as Jake was whisked away. A passing nurse noticed Mabel's blood-soaked shorts and did a double take, exclaiming that she needed care as well.

"No, it's all right," Mabel said quickly. "It's just a flesh wound."

"Looks like it could use some stitches," the nurse, a kindly young man, said, examining her leg.

"No," repeated Mabel. "It's not bleeding anymore; I'll put some butterfly bandages on it."

"It's your leg; I can't force you to accept help," he said. "But that wound will leave quite a scar. At least let me get some antibiotic ointment and bandage it up for you."

"I like scars," Mabel said. "But all right."

He brought the ointment and bandages to the waiting room and quickly applied them to the laceration.

"Don't mention to anyone that I did this," he said with a smile. "Or they'll slap a bill on you so fast your head will spin." He stood and patted her on the shoulder before leaving them alone again.

The doctor came into the room, face unreadable. Crossing to them, he put out his hand to Gina and she shook it.

"I'm Dr. Groves," he said. "And you are...?"

"I'm Gina Evans," she answered. "And this is Jane Ennis."

"Nice to meet you," he said, shaking Mabel's hand in turn.

"How are you related to the patient?"

"I'm a friend, and Jane here is his niece."

"Well, Ms. Ennis, your uncle has lost a lot of blood, which I'm sure you are aware of," the doctor said, turning to Mabel. "The bullet is lodged in his shoulder muscle and we're preparing to do surgery soon to remove it. The surgery shouldn't take more than an hour or so, but we're stabilizing him right now. I'll let you know as soon as the surgery is over how it went and how he is doing."

"Oh, but when can we see him?" Gina asked, eyes dangerously red.

"After surgery, if all goes well, you can see him then."

"Thank you doctor."

"You're welcome. The police will be in soon to get the story of how this happened. They have to investigate whenever there's a shooting, you understand."

"Yes, of course," Gina said. The doctor turned and strode from the room, leaving Mabel's heart quaking in her chest. The police. She considered running out the door, but knew it would only complicate matters.

Be cool she told herself sternly. *Be cool, and remember your story.*

"Are you okay, Jane?" Gina asked, seeing her face go pale beneath her tan.

"I'm okay; I just... I don't want to talk to the police."

"Just tell them exactly what you told me on the way over here. Everything will be fine." She reached out and took Mabel's hand in her own. They sat and tried to calm their individual minds and hearts, the air in the waiting room portentous with the accumulated anxiety of the people gathered there, each in their own private world of uncertainty and fear.

An hour passed, and then two. Gina and Mabel sipped at the complimentary coffee and tried to joke about how terrible it was. The TV blared the latest governmental fiasco and added another layer to the charged atmosphere.

Someone got up and snapped it off. Mabel sighed heavily.

"Somebody, please, come tell us something," she muttered.

Dr. Groves entered, face once again a mask of carefully practiced neutrality.

"Everything is fine," he said, as he crossed the room to them. Mabel felt the knot in her chest loosen, and bowed her head in ineffable relief. Gina brought her hands to her face as a sob escaped her.

"Took a little longer to dig the thing out than we predicted. There was quite a bit of damage to the muscle but we got him patched back together. He'll probably need some physical therapy to regain complete use of that arm again, but he's in excellent shape for a man his age and it shouldn't take too long."

"Thank you so much, doctor," Gina said, composing herself once more. "When might we see him?"

"Someone will come and get you once he's conscious again and we have his pain controlled." He shook their hands again and left. The two women looked at one another and Gina drew Mabel into a hug. Mabel suddenly felt profoundly weary.

"Excuse me, ma'am," a voice said behind her. She turned to see a uniform-clad policeman, and her heart did a terrible flip in her chest. "Are you Jane Ennis?"

Mabel nodded, unable to speak. He stuck his hand out and shook hers.

"I'm Officer Smith. Ms. Ennis, as you might have been told, we have to do a complete investigation into any shooting. You understand?" She nodded again.

"All right. Now, how are you related to Mr. Ennis?"

"I... I'm his niece," she said faintly, finding her voice.

"Can you tell me how this shooting happened?"

Mabel talked. She told of their vacation to the Dry Tortugas, of their brief meeting with Dan there, and their subsequent departure. She told of how they saw the disabled boat and went to help, of how Dan shot Jake and of the attempt upon her own life.

"You pulled out your pocketknife?" the officer said, somewhat incredulous.

"Yes. I pulled out my pocketknife and cut him

pretty good in the face. He fell backwards and I was able to push him overboard."

"You pushed him overboard?" the officer was no longer somewhat, but very incredulous.

"Yes. I pushed him overboard and then I turned on the motor and got the hell out of there."

"I see." The officer scribbled notes furiously, and then sat thoughtfully, chewing on the end of his pen. "What did you say the suspect's name was?"

"Dan. All he said was Dan. He didn't give a last name."

"Can you describe him?"

"Six feet tall, maybe. Normal sized. Mid-twenties, or thereabouts. He was dark blonde, but he had this big beard that covered most of his face. His beard was mostly red." More scribbling.

"And do you have any idea what his motivation was for trying to kill you both?"

"I think it must have something to do with the duffel bag full of money that he brought aboard right before he shot at us," she said. The officer dropped his pen and gaped at her.

"Duffel full of..."

"Of money, yes," Mabel finished for him.

"Well, Ms. Ennis," the officer said after some time. He seemed to be deciding just what to say. "I'm going to have to see that bag of money you described. Excuse me for a moment; I'll be right back."

"Okay."

The two women sat in silence again. Mabel leaned her head against Gina's shoulder and closed her eyes. When she opened them again, there were two uniformed officers in front of her.

"Ms. Ennis, this is detective Maloney. He's going to need to hear your story too."

"Okay," Mabel sighed. Again she told the story, with Officer Smith looking back and forth from her face to the detective's, chuckling at the look of amazement that soon overtook the detective's expression.

"See? I told you it was incredible!" He exclaimed. "Can you believe it?"

"I think we need to go see that bag of cash," the detective said. "Ms. Ennis, do you mind if you take us there now?" Mabel did mind, very much. She wanted to sit with Gina and wait until they could visit Jake, but the detective's face said that the question was less of a question than it seemed on the surface. She stood slowly.

"Yeah, let's go."

Back at *Stella Luna*, the detective took dozens of pictures of the boat, the destroyed radio, and the blood splatters in various places. He pried the bullets out of the paneling in the cabin and carefully placed them into zip lock baggies marked "evidence". The duffel bag was unzipped and its contents examined. When they were done, they carried the bag to the car and climbed back inside.

"Well, Ms. Ennis, you have had a rough twenty-four hours, haven't you?" Officer Smith said to her as the detective pulled out of the parking lot. "We'll take you back to the hospital now and hopefully you can see your uncle. We'll have to talk to him as well, just to be thorough."

Back at the hospital the nurse led them to the ICU, room 208, where Jake lay, shoulder bandaged, blood bag hanging next to him, looking pale but—to Mabel's mind—infinitely beautiful. Gina sat next to him, holding his hand. He opened his eyes, saw Mabel, and smiled.

"And there's my hero," he said softly as she crossed to him. She lay her head on his chest and listened to the beat of his heart, steady and calming, and dampened his gown with her tears.

15

Gina and Mabel left the hospital that night, after much discussion regarding whether one of them should stay with Jake or not.

"I'm not a child," he finally said, voice faint but firm. "You two will rest better at home, and I don't want either one of you to stay here with me."

"Are you sure, Jake?" Gina asked. "I thought–"

"You can come back tomorrow for a visit, but I'd rather you remember my ass the last time you saw it than hanging out of a hospital gown, for God's sake," he said.

"Okay then," she laughed, and kissed him. Mabel gave him a gentle hug. As they left the room, they were met by Officer Smith once more.

"I just wanted to warn you, Jane, that the press is outside waiting for you. They're going to yell a lot of questions at you and take a lot of pictures. You don't have to say anything or answer them at all. Do you understand?"

"Is there another way out?" she asked, freezing in trepidation.

"No, I'm afraid not," he answered. "The media is going nuts with this story. I came to tell you also that the man you encountered matches the description of a bank robber here in Florida. He and three accomplices knocked over a bank in Miami just three weeks ago. Cops caught the three friends, but he got away. There was a big manhunt out for him, didn't you guys see anything about it on the news?"

"Don't watch the news," Mabel said, feeling faint.

"Anyway, his name was Donald Freeman. He had a rap sheet about a mile long, and it is ugly. You're both very lucky to be alive."

"Yes." Mabel did not feel lucky at the moment.

"I can help you get past them, if you like. Ms. Evans, would you like to drive the car around so that Ms. Ennis here can get in quickly and get away?"

"Sure, I'll do that," Gina said, striding purposefully away.

"Ms. Ennis, just stay close to me and I'll get you to the car. I'm warning you that they'll probably be at your home as well, however. They manage somehow to find everything out, you know."

"I guess so," she said. "But what do they want?"

"Pictures, mostly. A soundbite or two to show on the evening news. This is a pretty big story, you understand? And you're the hero in it," he chuckled. "Frankly, I'd like your autograph."

They arrived at the doorway and peered out. Sure enough, the paparazzi was gathered there, waiting to pounce as soon as she showed her face. Gina pulled up with the car and Mabel took a deep breath.

"Ready," she said.

They plunged into the melee of people and cameras, and the shouting nearly deafened her. Flashbulbs blinded her and she kept her head down the whole way to the open car door, which she shut as quickly as possible once she was safely inside.

"Get me out of here," she muttered as Gina floored it, narrowly missing the most intrepid reporters.

"They're sure to be at the harbor too," Gina said. "What are we going to do?"

"I'm so tired; I just want to go to sleep," Mabel moaned.

"I'll park around the back of the bar and grill and you can run up to the apartment. Sleep as long as you want there. Will that work?"

"Yes, please," Mabel said.

Pulling into the parking spot, Mabel spied the news van and a small crowd of people milling around the dock's edge. She and Gina quietly shut the doors on the car and ran up the stairs that led to the apartment above the restaurant.

"We made it!" Gina exclaimed. "Now, here's the bathroom, and I'll pull out the couch bed. How about that? You can stay as long as you like."

"Thanks, Gina," Mabel said.

"You're very welcome. And Jane?"

"What?"

"Thank you. Thank you for getting back here safely with Jake. I don't know what I would have done if—"

"You're welcome, Gina," Mabel said, unwilling to entertain *what ifs*.

Gina left to attend to the bar and grill, and Mabel, alone at last, washed her face in the bathroom, curled up on the couch bed, and was fast asleep within moments.

16

"When are they going to release him?" Mabel asked Gina after five days had gone by. "I miss him a lot."

"I know you do. But he's got to stay another couple of days so they can guard against infection.

He's on some pretty heavy duty antibiotics, but they want to keep a close eye on him. Shouldn't be too much longer."

To occupy her time, Mabel took long walks around town, stopping in at the library for books and the small local market for sustenance. One day she wandered by a Panini shop and, answering the call of her ever-grumbling stomach, went in. The handsome young man at the counter exclaimed in surprise to see her.

"Jane, right?" he said. "It's Carl; remember me? From the beach? Geez, I haven't seen you in like forever. How have you been doing?"

"I'm hanging in there." He nodded.

"I saw you on the news. Crazy thing! That must have been really scary."

"It was."

"You're like, famous."

"I guess. I don't really want to talk about it."

"I understand. Anyway, want a sandwich? My treat? Let me make you one of my specialties."

Mabel nodded and he went to work. Before long she was biting into a delicious combination of salami, Portobello mushrooms and peppers mixed with provolone and mozzarella and doused in oil and vinegar. She wiped her mouth with a pile of napkins and smiled at him as he waited, expectant, for her reaction.

"Really good," she said, around her next enormous bite. "Messy, but really good."

He bowed deeply and went to wait on another customer.

"Hey, I get off here in about ten minutes," he said as she finished up. "Can I walk you home?"

She allowed that he could. Soon they were

strolling in the late afternoon sunshine, steaming hot and redolent with jasmine. When he reached for her hand, she did not protest, but thought to herself how very nice and warm it was in her own. At the bar and grill they sat in the shade of the awning and sipped on sweet tea that Gina brought out.

"So when's your uncle coming back?" he asked.

"Tomorrow," she said. "I've really missed him."

"I bet you were pretty worried."

"Yes. He's all I have," she said, and realized they were the most truthful words she had spoken in a very long time.

"It's just my mom and me," Carl was saying as he drained his glass. "My parents got divorced a long time ago, when I was really little. I don't remember my dad at all, and she says that's good. I guess he was a real ass."

"I'm sorry."

"Don't be. I'm not. My mom is great. You should come meet her some time, at my house. Hey, do you want to go to the movies on Friday? We could go see whatever you like."

"Like, on a date?" she said, stunned by the notion.

"Yeah, like a date," he laughed at her then, and she reddened.

"I've never been on a date before," she said. More truthfulness. It felt good, she noted.

"Wow, really? So will you come?"

"Yeah, okay."

"Awesome."

Carl walked her to *Stella Luna* and they sat on the deck with their feet dangling, watching the sun set in silence for a while and feeding bits of bread to the small fish that rose to the surface of the water with hungry mouths.

"I guess I'd better be going," Carl said finally, as the light began to fade. He leaned into her then, and took her face gently in his hands, turning her to him. With great tenderness he pressed his lips to hers, and she felt suddenly as though she was being reborn as an ordinary teenager with no dark past haunting her, just a teenaged girl getting her first real kiss from a boy on the deck of a boat. She scooted closer to him, and he put his arm around her as they continued. Finally, he broke away and sighed.

"That was... nice," Mabel said quietly. Carl laughed.

"Yeah, it was. Shall we do it again?"

They did. And it was even nicer. Carl smelled of soap and rising bread and sunshine, and he tasted slightly, pleasantly metallic. Eventually, however, when it was very dark indeed, he reluctantly disengaged himself, got up and walked off the boat to the dock, waving and disappearing around the corner of the bar. His slight swagger remained in Mabel's memory for a very long time as she lay in her bunk, drifting off to sleep, where the dreams that awaited her were all pleasant.

17

Jake was back at the sailboat the next day, though his recovery was destined to be long and arduous. The bullet had missed any bones, but the damage to the muscle was extensive and his arm remained in a sling. Still, he was itching to get back on the water, and with Mabel doing the heavy lifting, they took a test run to Mule Key and back without incident.

"You're good as new," she said to him, and he

laughed.

"Not quite," he said, wincing a little. "I still can't even tie a bowline with this blasted sling on."

"But you don't need to; we can still open up for business. I can sail; you just have to direct me."

"Maybe."

"Come on, why the hesitation?"

"Jane, there's just one thing I don't understand," he said, gazing hard into her eyes. She felt the import of the look, and tried to meet it with confidence. "How on earth did you get us back here, anyway? The navigation was completely obliterated by bullets. It cost $500 to fix it. There's no way—*no way*—a novice could have gotten us those last thirty miles on their own."

Mabel sat quietly, wondering how to answer. Was she crazy? Had Hemingway really visited her in the night and given her strength to go on? Or was it all a hallucination brought on by stress and blood loss? She didn't know what to think herself, but she cleared her throat and began.

"Hemingway came to me," she said.

"Jane, I'm ser–" he began, but stopped when he saw the look on her face. She spoke the next words in a rush.

"He did, Jake. He came to me, walking on the water. He cooked me fish and helped me sail. I couldn't have done it without him, just like you said. I don't know the north star from the sun."

Jake stood staring at her, mouth open slightly, trying to absorb the words she had said.

"Walking... on the water," he said slowly. "It must have been a hallucination, Jane. It must have–"

"But there was the fish that we ate together," she said, leaning forward earnestly. "I cleaned it up the next day. He fixed it for me. And the fact that we *did* get back here. A hallucination couldn't have done that."

"Maybe…" he said, running his hand through his hair until it stood on end.

"All I know is what I saw," she said. "And he was Hemingway, through and through, everything about him. I know it sounds crazy, Jake, but I'm *not* crazy. At least, not like that."

"I know you're not crazy, Jane," Jake said, shaking his head. "I don't know what to think. Not at all. But I'm glad you got us back somehow, or I'd have been a goner by the next evening. The doctor said so."

They sat on the deck that evening and ate grilled chicken from the bar, delivered to them by Gina herself, who dropped a kiss upon Jake's cheek as she left. Jake asked Mabel what she had been doing besides hiding from the police while he was in the hospital.

"Well…" she said, flushing a little. "I have a date on Friday night."

"You what?" Jake coughed on his chicken and looked at her, almost more incredulous than he had been when she told him about Hemingway.

"I have a date," she repeated. "With this guy I met. His name is Carl."

"But Jane, what do you know about him? I mean, where did you meet him? How do you know he's okay?"

She laughed at his concern. "I met him at South Beach on my first day off. He's nice. He works at the Panini place and goes to the community college. He's studying to be an EMT."

"Okay," he said, his forehead still deeply furrowed. "What are you going to do on this date?"

"Go to a movie. Get something to eat, I guess. What do people do on dates?"

"Just that I guess. Plus some other things, sometimes. Jane, are you sure you'll be okay?"

"I'm sure, Jake. I'll be fine."

Friday dawned rainy and dark, and so Mabel set about cleaning the cabin of the boat, a ministration it was deeply in need of. She scrubbed the blood splatters off the walls and stripped the sheets off the bunks, stuffing them one at a time into the tiny washing machine and clipping them to the lifeline when they were done, hoping the rain would hold off long enough to give them a chance to dry.

"This place is going to be ship-shape when you're done," Jake joked, looking up from the Agatha Christie novel he was reading. She stuck her tongue out at him and went into the bathroom to wipe it down with disinfectant. When she was finished she went to stand on the deck, antsy and unsure of what to do next.

Crossing to the bar and grill, she sat down and ordered a club sandwich, waving at Gina in the bar area, but once the food arrived she could only eat a few bites. Her stomach was jumpy and nervous and excited and happy all at once at the prospect of seeing Carl again.

"Ms. Ennis?" a voice said by her elbow.

"What?" she said, turning.

A slight man with a carefully groomed goatee stood on the boardwalk with a kindly smile on his face. He was dressed in business-casual clothing and looked out of place among the bathing suit and shorts-clad set that frequented the area.

"Jane Ennis?"

"Yes," she said, the blood pulsing loudly in her

ears. She looked furtively around for help from Gina, but she wasn't in sight. The small man moved closer and put his hand out.

"I'm David Hunter; I'm a reporter for *Hello* Magazine, maybe you've heard of it?"

She had heard of it; it was on all the newsstands and grocery store check-outs.

"If you are familiar at all with our magazine, then you know that we do human interest stories in every edition. We'd very much like to do one on you."

"I... I'd really rather not," she said.

"Are you sure? It would be a very complimentary piece; all about how you fought off your attacker and saved the life of your uncle. Real woman-power stuff."

"No," she shook her head. "I really don't want to."

"Okay, well, it's not my job to force anybody to be in our magazine. Can I just ask you a few questions?"

"Okay," she said, hoping to get rid of him quickly.

"Your family comes from Miami, right? Are you an only child?"

"Yes."

"And you're eighteen years old?"

"Yes."

"Funny, you don't really look eighteen." Mabel shrugged.

"Mr. Ennis is your uncle on your father's side, or your mother's?"

"Father's."

"Okay, well, I'm sorry you don't want to do the piece. I'll be going now. Enjoy your afternoon, okay?"

"Okay, thanks."

He strode away, but Mabel saw him stop at

Stella Luna and speak for a few minutes to Jake before he moved on and disappeared from sight. When she went back to the boat, she asked him about it.

"He wanted to interview me, but I declined, to say the least," Jake said. "I don't know when they'll finally get tired of this story and move on. They'll want to make a movie next."

Mabel sighed. "It's only been a week yet."

"At any rate, don't let it ruin your date tonight, Jane," he said, interpreting her gloomy look correctly. "I'm sure something else newsworthy will happen soon and they'll lose interest in us and our bad-guy ass-kicking skills. Or rather, *your* bad-guy ass-kicking skills."

"I hope so," she answered.

At five o'clock Carl arrived, striding down the boardwalk, looking resplendent in jeans and a simple button down shirt, and Mabel's heart thudded in her chest at the sight of him. She had bought a new sundress from a local boutique just for the occasion, and she came up from below deck to greet him.

"Hey Jane," Carl said, smiling broadly as he stood on the dock looking up at her. "You look pretty."

"Hey Carl," she answered in what she hoped was a casual tone. "So do you."

"You coming aboard?" Jake said, coming around the helm and stretching out his hand to the young man.

"Sir," said Carl, taking his hand and shaking it firmly as he stepped onto the deck. "I saw you on the news. How's the shoulder?"

"Oh, it's healing. Slowly but surely, slowly but surely."

"I was telling Jane that you guys are celebrities around here," he said. "You're famous."

Jake laughed heartily and shook his head.

"What movie are you going to see, then?" he asked.

"I thought we'd go see that thriller. The one about the kid with special powers, you know?"

"Oh yeah; I heard that was good."

"Well, we'd better get a move on I guess." Carl held his hand out to Mabel and she took it. They climbed down from the boat and waved to Jake as they disappeared. Jake stood for a moment and then crossed to the bar, where he found Gina. She served him his whiskey and he winked at her.

"Kid went to a movie," he said. "Not sure how long she'll be gone. Not sure what to do with myself. What did I used to do before she came along?"

"I can think of a thing or two," Gina said with a small smile.

At the movie, Carl put his arm around Mabel's shoulders and she leaned into him. The last movie Mabel had gone to the theater for was a Disney film when she was seven and living with a family of five. They had gone for a birthday, she remembered, although not her own. As the opening credits rolled, she looked up at Carl.

"Thank you," she said.

"It's barely started yet," he laughed.

"Still. Thank you."

"You're welcome," he said, and kissed her on the nose.

The movie was fantastic, Mabel thought, with plenty of character development mixed with action, and she thoroughly enjoyed herself. When it was over she joined with several audience members and applauded.

"That was wonderful," she sighed as they walked out. "And a happy ending, too. I really loved it."

"And I loved watching you love it," Carl remarked. "You were more entertaining than the film itself."

"Really?" she said, blushing. "Should I be embarrassed?"

"No," he said, taking her hand as they walked. "Definitely not. What do you want to eat?"

"How about pizza?" she said.

"How about it," he nodded. "I know a great place; brick oven, coal fired pies. Excellent. Let's go."

They walked several blocks to the restaurant, where they ordered a large pepperoni and black olive and made short work of it.

"So when will you go back to school?" Carl asked. "To study marine biology, you said?"

Mabel shrugged, and thought quickly of how to turn the conversation around.

"I don't know. I'm really enjoying Jake's boat right now. I said I'd only take a year, but I'm thinking maybe I'll do more than that. What about you? When do you graduate and be an EMT?"

"Just one more year," he said.

"Maybe I should do that too," she said. "It would be nice to be able to help people when they're hurt."

"Yeah, it's pretty interesting stuff to learn about," he said. "Though not everyone is cut out for it. If you're squeamish about blood and stuff, I mean."

"Oh yeah," Mabel said with a toss of her head. "I'm definitely not squeamish."

"I guess not," he laughed. "Carving up bad guys is your superpower, right?"

"That's right."

"Want to go to my house?" he asked. "You could meet my mom."

"Sure," she said. He paid the tab and they walked back to the theater to his car and climbed in.

At his house Mabel met Carl's mother Susan, a tall, thin woman with long blond hair and the same piercing blue eyes as her son.

"I'm so glad to meet you, Jane," she said. "Carl has talked about you nonstop." Mabel blushed.

"Jane, do you want a drink or anything?" Carl asked, opening up the fridge. "We've got soda and stuff."

"Sure. I'll take one."

He handed her a Dr. Pepper and they went to the living room, where he turned on the television. The news was on, and with a shock, Mabel saw her own face projected there. Pictures of her taken with a telephoto lens, grainy but recognizable, littered the screen.

"Oh hey," Carl said. "There you are again."

Jane Ennis, the beautiful blond reporter was saying, *who slew notorious bank robber Donald Freeman and saved her uncle's life in a daring high-seas adventure, has fast become a local legend here in Key West. But is she really who she says she is? Stay tuned for the rest of the story...*

Mabel snatched up the remote, which seemed unreasonably slippery in her grasp, and fumbled to hit the off button. The television went off with a snap, but the damage was done.

Her heart was fluttering like a bird in a snare, and she thought she might be sick to her stomach.

"Jane?" Carl was asking from very far away. "Jane, are you all right? What were they talking about?"

"I need to go home," she said faintly. "I... I need to go right now. Please."

"Sure, sure you can," he said, standing. "Come on, I'll take you."

She stood, but her legs felt like they belonged to someone else, and she walked woodenly to the door. Susan called a good-bye, but she didn't hear. They drove back to the harbor in silence, Carl casting worried glances her way.

"Jane," he said when they arrived, before she could bolt out the door. "I don't know what that was all about, but I just wanted to say I had a really nice time with you tonight. I hope I can see you again."

Mabel nodded slightly and opened the door, breathing great gulps of the night air and trying to calm her racing thoughts.

"Things are going to change a lot now," she choked out. "But I've loved my time with you."

He leaned over and kissed her then, wiping away the tears that tracked down her face.

"Can't you just tell me what it's all about?"

"I'm sorry," she sobbed, and ran for the safety of *Stella Luna*, and Jake.

18

Jane Ennis was once more *Mabel Banner*, fifteen year old foster kid, runaway from Oklahoma, and person of interest in the slaying of one Ms. Gail Thomas.

"Jane... I mean, Mabel," Jake said as the authorities came to take her back to Oklahoma. "Write me. Please. I gave you my email; use it. Okay? Let me know how you're doing?"

She nodded, not trusting herself to speak.

She had already cried more than should have been physically possible, and she was exhausted.

"Yes. Mabel, let us know, whatever happens," Gina said. They hugged her, and Mabel clung to Jake.

"Just be strong," he whispered into her ear, heart breaking for the girl he had only just begun to get to know. "You can do this. You're the strongest person I've ever known."

Mabel was strong. She stood trial and recited the abuses she had suffered in a clear, even voice that had the jurors marveling at her composure. The noxious room behind the store had long since been discovered, so with corroboration from the other foster daughters who testified that Gail had made Mabel "work the store", the verdict of *not guilty by reason of self-defense* was not difficult to obtain.

She was strong when the press asked their probing questions, when the media demanded to know all about her former whereabouts and what she had done with her time. She spoke in a calm, detached manner of Jake and *Stella Luna* and Gina and Key West, and didn't shed a tear when they asked if she missed them.

She was strong when they placed her in her new foster home, with a middle-class couple by the name of Bob and Julie, who had no children but two French bulldogs who made her smile with their antics and unconditional affection.

She was strong when she started school again, startling her literature teachers with her extensive knowledge of Hemingway, and pulling straight A's. She studied hard, kept to herself, and made no friends. She took up sketching and drew many fine pictures of *Stella Luna*, the ocean, and Jake.

She was strong when she went to therapy and

told the counselors of the fears and nightmares that plagued her nights, her compulsive need to be alone and the urges that whispered to her that she was damaged goods and that cutting was the release she needed. She was put on antianxiety meds, and they helped. Most of the time.

She was strong when she wrote to Jake, making sure to emphasize the good that was happening so as not to worry him, telling him that she was doing fine. She sent the emails often, and was never happier than when she received one back from him. He told her funny stories of his new first mate, who was worthless and smoked pot constantly, and of how much he missed her.

She was strong, and brave, and good, and she held her dreams close to her heart and shared them with no one but the bulldogs when they sat on her lap and fawned for attention. They looked at her with their laughing faces and whined when she scratched their bellies and licked her tears away before they could even fall.

19

Jake stepped off *Stella Luna* and headed for the bar, where Gina met him with a kiss and a glass of whiskey. It was an achingly beautiful evening in Key West, late spring, and the weather was turning out days like pearls, each one more transcendent than the last.

"How was your day?" she asked.

"Just long," he answered, sipping at the amber liquid and smiling. "You're a sight for sore eyes, though."

"Oh pshaw," she said.

"Lost my first mate again," he said with a sigh.

"Again!" she exclaimed.

"Yep. Just couldn't handle the hours, I guess. Called in well this morning right before my first gig."

"I guess some things never change," a voice said behind him. He turned to see a stunning young woman with a radiant smile standing with a suitcase in her hand. "Mabel!" he cried, and jumped off the stool to wrap her in a hug. Gina came around the side of the bar and enveloped her as well. "You didn't say you were coming!"

"I wanted to surprise you. I hope that's okay."

"Okay? It's fantastic!"

"You hungry?" Gina asked, motioning for her to sit down.

"When am I not?" Mabel laughed, sitting. Gina brought sandwiches and sweet tea and she and Jake sat with the girl, peppering her with questions.

"I can't believe it's been three years already," Jake said, shaking his head. "How's it feel to be out of the foster care system?"

"Wonderful," she answered, between bites of sandwich.

"Bob and Julie are great people; they treated me really well, but I was ready to be on my own. More than ready."

"I guess so," Gina said. "You've already lived through more than most people do their whole lives."

"And what are your plans, Mabel?" Jake asked. "Are you going to college?"

"Already enrolled in Gulf Coast University," she said, nodding. "I'm going to study Literature. I'll only be a few hours away."

"Oh honey, that's just wonderful," Gina exclaimed.

"Yeah, that's great," Jake said. "What about this

summer? Do you have a place to stay? More to the point, do you want a job?"

"You know it," she said. "I have only one request."

"What is it?"

She drew from her purse an object and held it out to Jake.

"A stamp in my passport."

"You got it, Mabel," he said, grinning. "You got it."

Epilogue

The young woman in the yellow sundress strolled down the Cuban street, hat in hand, taking in the architecture of the place and feeling the endless weight of history all around her. Men stopped what they were doing and gazed after her as she passed, but she ignored their stares and the occasional catcall.

Climbing the steps to *La Casa Del Habanos,* she bought a box of ten Cohiba cigars. The lady behind the counter smiled as she wrapped it in paper and put it in a plastic bag.

"Your man is sure to like," she said softly.

"Gracias," the young woman answered.

Catching a taxi back to the Hemingway Marina, she stepped onto the deck of the sailboat and greeted the man waiting there.

"Find everything you wanted?" he asked.

"Sure did," she said.

Later, sitting on the deck of the boat, they puffed on the redolent cigars, watching the smoke drift lazily into the night sky.

"How do you feel?" he asked, putting his arm around her.

"Intoxicated," she said, smiling. "By the romance of the unusual."

"Who said that?" he said.

"Who else? Hemingway."

"I should have known."

They sat in silence then, feeling the gentle rock of the boat, and the vastness of the gulf before them.

"We made it," she said.

"Yes we did."

Lightning flashed over the water as a storm raged to the west.

"Are you going to be ready to leave tomorrow?" he asked.

"Sure. I've gotten all I wanted. I suppose we need to get back to work."

"I suppose we do."

"Jake?" she asked.

"Yes, Mabel?"

"You're the best thing that ever happened to me."

"Well."

Silence again. It was comfortable, just sitting together with their legs dangling above the dark water, finishing their cigars. A gentle rain began to patter down around them and Jake got up to go into the cabin, but Mabel still sat, face lifted to the sky, free and unafraid.

Jennifer Wilson lives in Texas with her husband and seven of her thirteen children. When she is not negotiating peace treaties between the warring factions residing beneath her roof, she enjoys writing and playing the banjo. Occasionally she hides in the closet and drinks whiskey while contemplating the meaning of the universe. She has published four books of poetry and two novels, blogs at crazyreal.net.

Thank you to the Wapshott Press sponsors, supporters, and Friends of the Wapshott Press.

Kit Ramage
Muna Deriane
James Wilson
Rachel Livingston
Kathleen Warner
Robert Earle and Mary Azoy
Kathleen Bonagofsky
Suzanne Siegel
Phil Temples
James and Rebecca White
Richard Whittaker
Debbie Jones and Steven Acker
Cynthia Henderson
Nancy Lilly
Jennifer Bentson
Patricia Nerad
Ann Siemens
Elaine Padilla
Laurel Sutton
John Grigor Bell

The Wapshott Press is a 501(c)(3) not-for-profit enterprise publishing work by emerging and established authors and artists. We publish books that should be published. We are very grateful to the people who believe in our plans and goals, as well as our hopes and dreams. Our new website is at www. WapshottPress.org. Donations gratefully accepted at www.Donate.WapshottPress.org.